Snowfall

BY COURTNEY LYMAN

Other books by Courtney Lyman

Holliday Hotel
Resolution Room
Book 2 arriving in February 2017

KW Consulting Series
Best Laid Plans
Smell the Roses
Dress for Success
Always a Bridesmaid

Christmas Novellas
Christmas Angel
Snowfall

Dedicated to my sister-in-law,

Rachel Lyman

"And the angel said to them, "Fear not, for behold, I bring you good news of great joy that will be for all the people."
- Luke 2:10

"...not neglecting to meet together, as is the habit of some, but encouraging one another, and all the more as you see the Day drawing near."
- Hebrews 10:25

The Thief

Snowfall was belying its name this year. Even though it was the first week of December, they hadn't received more than a dusting of snow. It had been chilly, but there hadn't been much precipitation. Snowfall was a small town. It mostly consisted of a grocery store, a feed store, a gas station, a couple of restaurants, a bar, a vet, and the police station. Few people actually lived in the town, but the town supported the families that ranched around it.

Dylan Thompson got out of his truck and surveyed the town. He had lived here his whole life except for when he left for college. While he was in his junior year, his dad had unexpectedly passed away, so Dylan had quit school and come home. His family had owned the feed store for generations, and he knew his mom was going to need him to keep it going. He had hoped to eventually finish his schooling, but it just hadn't been possible. Not that he regretted his decision. He loved his mom, and he knew that she was appreciative of his help.

Dylan sighed and headed into the feed store. He waved to his employees as he headed to the back office. A group of ranchers were clustered around talking about the lack of snow and what that would mean for them in the spring. He

1

settled into the routine of the day and tried not to think of how similar this day would be to every other day since he had taken over the store from his dad. Thompson's Feed was a local institution. It had been around since the town had been founded. He couldn't imagine it being turned over to someone else. At the same time, he hated the monotony of the job.

The morning dragged on until a rap on the door interrupted his gloomy thoughts. He shook his head and blamed the gray skies for his mood. "Come in," he said, forcing a welcoming smile on his face.

"Do you have any free time for your old mom?" A small woman with short gray hair and a twinkle in her eye popped her head in the office.

Dylan laughed and stood up. He quickly crossed the small office to give his mom a hug. "I always have time for you, Mom. And I'd hurt anyone else who called you 'old'."

His mom smiled at him affectionately. "And that's one reason why I love you so much. How about having lunch with your mother?"

Dylan glanced at the pile of work on his desk, but then heard his stomach growl. He chuckled. "I guess I hadn't noticed how hungry I am."

His mom shook her head. "Just like every other day. Come on. They'll be fine without you for an hour." Dylan grabbed his jacket and followed her through the store. Jean Thompson may be petite, but when she said "jump", you asked "how high". She had ruled their home firmly, but fairly. Her husband had loved her devotedly, and her heart had broken when he had died. It was only the support of their only child that had kept her going after his death. Eventually she had been able to emerge from her grief, although Dylan knew that she still counted time by how long it had been since her husband's death.

Together they walked down the street to a diner and stepped inside out of the brisk air. After getting seated and placing their order, Dylan placed his hands on the table. "Okay, Mom. What's on your mind?"

Jean fiddled with her napkin and glanced down at her hands. "What makes you think there's anything on my mind? Can't I just want to have lunch with my son?"

"You could, but you didn't." Dylan leaned forward. "Come on, Mom. I know you too well. Now, what's going on?"

Jean sighed. She compressed her lips and then took a deep breath. "Christmas is coming."

"Yes, it is. Just like it comes every year." Dylan couldn't imagine what his mom had on her mind.

"Your aunt wants me to come visit her for Christmas this year in Arizona," Jean blurted out.

"That sounds like a wonderful idea. You haven't seen Aunt Paige in years." Dylan didn't know why she had been so reluctant to tell him that. It sounded like wonderful news to him.

Jean twisted her paper napkin around her finger. "If I go, you'll be all alone for Christmas."

Dylan leaned back in the booth. So that was it. The waitress came and dropped off their food before disappearing. After a brief prayer, Dylan looked at his mom before picking up his burger. "That's what you're worried about? I'll be fine."

Jean shook her head and the worried look wouldn't leave her face. She picked at her salad. "I don't know." She brightened and looked up for a moment. "Maybe you could come with me."

Dylan immediately shook his head. "You know I can't leave the store without one of us here."

"Sure you can! What's the point of having managers if

3

you never leave them in charge? I swear that store is going to kill you, just like it killed your father." Jean blinked back tears.

Dylan sighed. "Mom, it's not that. I've already told Wayne he could have the holidays off to go visit his family in Nebraska which leaves Zach, our new employee who's still learning the ropes. I can't leave him in charge by himself just yet."

Jean tapped her nails on the table. "Maybe I should wait until next year. Zach will be able to hold down the fort for you, and you can come with me."

Dylan popped a french fry in his mouth. "I don't want you to postpone this because of me."

"I wouldn't be happy there knowing you were alone on Christmas day. Paige will understand." She glanced up at him briefly. "Now if you weren't alone . . . if you had a girlfriend, or something . . ."

"Mom, we've been over this before." Dylan sighed.

Jean held up her hands. "I know, I know." She pointed her fork at him. "Still it'd be nice to see you settle down, maybe give me some grandkids."

Dylan laughed. "I know, I know. But it's not like Snowfall is crawling with young, single women, let alone any that I would like to be with."

Jean shook her head. "You're too picky. What about Hayley Carter?"

Dylan couldn't keep the disgust off his face. "Absolutely not! No, I'm not being picky. I just want to be with someone that I can see spending the rest of my life with. I haven't met anyone like that yet." He stuck a french fry in Jean's face. "And deep down you want that as well."

Jean sighed. "I know. I just wish God would bring someone for you."

"Until then, I'm content as I am." Dylan sipped his

4

soda. "So, are you going to Aunt Paige's for Christmas?"

"I don't think I can," Jean replied sadly.

Dylan put his hand on top of his mom's. "You can, and you will. Let Aunt Paige know you're coming. We'll celebrate together when you get home."

Jean smiled sadly. "I guess it will be okay."

"It will, Mom. I'm a grown man. I can take care of myself." Dylan paid the check and the two stood up. He placed his arm around her shoulders. "Go, and have a wonderful visit."

"All right, Dylan. You're probably right." They walked back to the feed store. "I know you'll be fine, but I'll miss you."

Dylan hugged her. "I'll miss you, too, but I want you to have a wonderful time with your sister." He headed into the feed store, and Jean got in her car to go home. As soon as he walked in, Zach caught his eye and then nodded toward the back. Dylan frowned and headed toward his manager. "What's going on?"

"Maybe nothing," Zach admitted. He nodded at a kid that was standing in a corner. "He's been hanging around for a while. Isn't really doing much, but something tells me that he needs an eye kept on him." He kept his voice low, but Dylan could tell that he was genuinely concerned.

Dylan looked over at the kid. He seemed young, possibly eleven or twelve. He kept shifting his stance , and his eyes kept darting over everything. "What do you think he's up to? It seems like he's nervous about something."

"That's what I was thinking, too," Zach admitted. "I don't know what he'd be trying to do in a feed store though. If this was the convenience store, I'd be sure he was getting ready to shoplift something, but what would he take here?"

Dylan shook his head. It didn't make any sense, but

it was obvious that the boy was uncomfortable. "Let's keep an eye on him, but try not to make him more uncomfortable. Maybe if he lets his guard down, he'll show us his hand."

Zach nodded and went to stock some shelves. Dylan decided that he could use a second pair of eyes and started doing some inventory. It wasn't long before he noticed the boy slip near the dog supplies. Dylan kept his eyes on the boy so he noticed the moment the boy grabbed a bag of dog food and stuffed it under his jacket before heading to the door. Dog food? Dylan started following the boy, but he wasn't careful enough. The boy glanced over his shoulder and fear showed on his face. He grabbed the bag of food tighter and started to run. Dylan took off after him, and it didn't take him long to catch the boy. He held him tightly as Zach came out the door. Dylan grabbed the bag of dog food and handed it to Zach. "Here. Put this back. I'll take care of the kid."

Zach nodded. "Want me to call the police?"

"No, I don't think that will be necessary." The boy had stopped struggling and hung his head in defeat. "I think we can take care of this on our own." Dylan marched the boy over to his truck and placed him inside. He had no worries that the boy had a weapon. Whatever he might be, Dylan was sure he wasn't dangerous. "I'll take him home. Maybe having a discussion with his parents will be enough."

The Confession

Dylan started the truck and turned to face the kid. "So where do you live?" The boy had his arms crossed across his chest and was staring sullenly out the window. "If you don't want to tell me, that's fine. I'll just take you to the police. I'm sure they can get you home, but that will probably be a lot rougher for you." Dylan shifted his truck into gear.

"I live at Golden Creek Ranch," the boy mumbled.

Dylan smiled. He figured the boy would rather have him take him home than the police. He set the truck in motion. Having lived here his entire life, Dylan knew exactly where the ranch was located. He hadn't been out there since Ray Golden had died, but he'd heard it had passed to Ray's granddaughter. This must be her son.

The rumors around town weren't very favorable towards the new owner. Dylan had never believed them, but now that her son had tried to steal from his store he wondered if maybe he should give them more credence.

He glanced toward the boy and wondered if maybe the ranch was falling on hard times. Why else would he steal dog food? "I'm Dylan Thompson." Dylan decided that he'd get the conversation going. Maybe the boy would open up to him. "I own the feed store."

The boy continued to stare out the window. Dylan

sighed. "I've lived here all my life. I knew your great grandpa well. He was a good man." He saw the boy shrug. Dylan frowned. "How do you like living on the ranch?"

"It's okay," the boy muttered.

Dylan shook his head. "When I was your age, I couldn't stay away from my friend's ranch. I loved the horses and the chores. When I was old enough your great grandpa would hire me for chores occasionally. I wanted nothing more than to own a ranch and be a cowboy."

The boy looked over at him for a moment with something like disbelief. "So what happened?"

Dylan felt a small thrill that the boy had continued the conversation. "I went to college and was studying to be a rancher when my dad died. I had to come home and take over the business."

"Why couldn't your mom do it?"

Dylan looked at the boy with a sense of wonder. "No one's ever asked me that before," he admitted. "My mom sort of had a – well, I guess a break down would best describe it – after my dad died. She wasn't in the frame of mind to handle the business, and it's been in our family since the town was settled. It would have broken her heart even more to lose it."

The boy shrugged and turned back to the passing scenery. "If she cared about it she should have taken care of it. And if she cared about you, she should have let you do what you wanted to do."

"Is that what your mom does? Let you do whatever you want." Dylan couldn't help, but ask the question.

He saw a shadow cross the boy's face. "No." Dylan sensed that the boy had shut down. He supposed he shouldn't have asked the question. Boys could be protective of their mothers. Look at all he had done for his own mom.

"Well, maybe I cared more about my mom than I cared

about having a ranch." Dylan hoped the boy would start talking again, but he remained silent and he knew that the boy had closed the door of communication between them.

The remainder of the trip passed in silence. He pulled into the long gravel driveway of the ranch and pulled in front of the two story house. He guessed that the boy's mom heard the tires on the gravel because the screen door opened and a woman stepped out onto the porch. She was slender with long chestnut hair. She pulled a jacket on over her sweater as she watched her son and Dylan step out of the truck. The boy ran up the steps and tried to slip by his mom, but she grabbed his hand as he went by. Dylan knew that the boy could easily have pulled away from his mom, but he allowed his mom to stop him.

"Eric, where have you been?" she asked, the worry evident in her voice. Eric shrugged his shoulders. Dylan saw the woman's eyes narrow. "That's not an answer. Unless you were knocked unconscious you know where you've been. Where was it?"

Eric glanced at Dylan who remained at the bottom of the porch steps. He rolled his eyes and sighed, apparently deciding that it would come out eventually. "I was at the feed store."

"The feed store?" The woman was obviously surprised by the answer. "What were you doing at the feed store?"

Eric looked down at his feet and scuffed them against the wood of the porch.

"Maybe I can help with that," Dylan stepped in. Eric looked at him in panic. "It seems he needed to pick up some dog food." Dylan had thought that he was helping by not pointing out that the dog food had been stolen, but the look on Eric's face told him that he had messed things up for him.

"Dog food?" The woman looked between Dylan and

9

Eric. "Why would you need to get dog food? We don't have a dog." She looked at Eric for a moment and then added with more emphasis, "We don't have a dog, do we, Eric?"

Eric wouldn't meet his mother's gaze as he shrugged his shoulders.

The woman sighed. "Go get the dog." Eric shuffled off with his shoulders slumped. The woman turned her attention back to Dylan and headed down the porch steps with her hand outstretched.

"I'm sorry. I don't believe we've met. I'm Cassidy Golden."

"Dylan Thompson." Dylan shook her hand firmly and stepped back.

"Thanks for bringing Eric home. I'm sure it was an inconvenience for you."

Now that he was closer, he could see that Cassidy had green eyes, but that they had a look of strain about them. Her mouth was full and soft, but he got the feeling that she didn't smile often. "Well, I sort of had to." Dylan stumbled over the words. In the silence of the truck, he had made his speech ready to lay into a mother who obviously let her son run wild, but now that he had seen her with Eric he knew somehow that those ideas were simply misconceptions. In the way that Eric had respectfully stayed when his mom had grabbed his hand, in the way that he had obeyed when his mom had told him to get the dog, it all showed that Cassidy was not a lax mother.

Her eyes narrowed now. "Had to?" She took a deep breath. "What did he do?" She asked the question softly and seemed to hold her breath as she waited for his answer.

Dylan looked at the ground. He knew she needed to know, but he hated having to tell her. "He didn't intend on paying for the dog food."

"He tried to steal it, you mean." Cassidy sighed softly

10

and shook her head. "I'm so sorry, Mr. Thompson. Thank you for not taking him to the police."

Dylan shrugged. "It didn't seem like he was someone who did this routinely."

"He didn't want to tell me about the dog so he didn't have money to buy food for it." A sharp bark drew her attention. Eric was returning with a beautiful border collie on a leash. The dog leapt next to the boy with excitement. When they reached the porch the collie sat next to Eric. "Who is this?" Cassidy asked.

Eric's expression was hopeful. "Her name is Carlie. My friend is moving to the city and they're going to be in an apartment so his mom told him he had to find her a home or she'd put her in the shelter." Eric's words tumbled over themselves in his eagerness to convince him mom. "So I had to take her."

Cassidy's eyes had softened, but at the last sentence, they hardened again. "No, you didn't have to – especially not behind my back. You disobeyed me, lied to me and now you tried to steal to cover your lie. When was it going to end?"

Dylan knew he should be going, but somehow he couldn't leave the drama that was unfolding before him. He was getting a glimpse into this little family, and it intrigued him.

Eric shrugged. "I was afraid you'd say no." He kept his eye on the dog. Carlie seemed to sense the tension and scooted closer to Cassidy. With a whine, she licked Cassidy's hand and Dylan saw her eyes soften again.

"Eric, you know this can't go unpunished. This behavior is not okay." She took the leash from his hand. "Go to your room. I'll be up as soon as I finish deciding what to do about this." She watched as Eric slowly mounted the steps and entered the house. She turned back to Dylan. "I don't suppose you know someone who needs a dog?" She rubbed Carlie's ears absently. "I can't let him keep her after what he did."

"Sorry, I don't. But if I hear of anyone I'll let you know." Dylan stuck his hands in his jean pockets. "I suppose I'd better go." Cassidy nodded her head. He could tell that her mind was far away, most likely trying to decide the best discipline for the crime. "If you need anything, just let me know." He didn't know what had prompted him to make the offer, or what she would need that he could supply, but he knew he meant it. Again she nodded. She headed up the porch steps, and Dylan knew that he had been dismissed. She probably wouldn't give him another thought. For some reason, that idea bothered him.

The Sentencing

Cassidy allowed Carlie to follow her inside. She got a dish of water and set it on the kitchen floor and wasn't surprised when the dog eagerly lapped it up. "Oh Carlie! What am I going to do with you?" The dog looked up when she heard her name and thumped her tail on the floor. Cassidy scratched her black and white fur before heading up the stairs to confront Eric. She tapped on his bedroom door, but didn't wait for a response before opening the door. Eric was sitting on his bed with his head resting on his knees, his face buried in his arms. Cassidy sat on the edge of the bed and sighed.

"Eric, what did you think would happen?" For the life of her, Cassidy didn't know how her son thought she wouldn't eventually figure this out.

Eric shrugged sulkily.

"That's not an answer. And if you can't give me answers, I'm going to have to add more to your punishment."

Eric raised his head, and Cassidy was surprised to see that his eyes were red rimmed from holding back tears. "I guess I hoped that once you met Carlie, you'd love her as much as I did and let me keep her."

Cassidy shook her head. "Here's the deal. You went behind my back, you lied to me, you deliberately disobeyed

13

me, and then you tried to steal something. You realize that to cover up your initial offense, you kept adding more to it, don't you? There is absolutely no possible way that I can let you keep that dog. I would be teaching you that if you just manipulate the situation, you can get what you want, and that's just not true." Eric blinked back tears, and Cassidy had to steel herself. "The sad part is, that Carlie is a sweet dog, and I might have let you keep her if you had come to me and just asked."

"You would not! You kept telling me that I couldn't get a dog until I proved that I could take care of one. But how can prove that if I don't have one to take care of?" Anger seemed to ooze out of every part of him.

Cassidy looked at him for a long moment. "Do you think you proved you were capable of taking care of Carlie now?" Eric was silent, but she could tell he was thinking about it. "Let me help you. You had to keep the poor dog hidden. I'm assuming, you kept her tied up in the barn. She needs exercise, but she wasn't allowed to run. You couldn't feed her, so you tried to steal food. When I gave her water just now, she lapped it up so greedily that I can only assume that you've forgotten to give her water as well."

"Okay, I get it," Eric stopped her.

"Do you? Then you'll understand that the first thing I have to do is find a new home for Carlie." Eric started to protest. "No, you proved to me that I was right to say no to getting you a dog. Now you have to start over." Eric put his head back down on his arms, but he stopped grumbling. "That only covers your manipulation of the situation though." Cassidy shifted on the bed so that she faced Eric better. "You're also grounded for two weeks for lying to me and disobeying. One week for each one."

Eric's head shot up and his eyes were wide. "But Mom! There are Christmas parties coming up, and I'll miss them!"

"Yep, you sure will. Sad, isn't it? If only you had made a better choice." Eric rolled his eyes and put his head back down, but Cassidy wasn't done yet. "But you still have one more offense that I haven't mentioned." Eric turned his head to peak out at his mom. Cassidy could see the fear in his eyes just from the little bit she could glimpse of his face. "You tried to steal from Mr. Thompson."

"He didn't do anything about it! Why should you?" Eric's panic was clearly revealed on his face.

"Because the next time you try to steal, you may not find someone as nice as Mr. Thompson. I need to make sure that you've learned not to do it again."

"I won't, Mom! I promise!" Eric gripped Cassidy's arm.

"There's two options for you. The first is to go to Mr. Thompson and offer to work for him for free for the month of December."

Eric's face paled. "No, Mom, please. I'm too embarrassed."

"The other option is to go to the police and tell them what you did and ask for community service."

Cassidy didn't think Eric's eyes could get any wider, but they did. "Mom! You wouldn't!"

"I would. I want you to grow into a godly young man, and right now your actions are showing me that you are on a bad path. I can't let you continue in that direction."

"You're afraid I'm going to be like Dad, aren't you?" Eric accused.

Cassidy took a breath. "I'm afraid that one day you will make poor choices that will have worse consequences than this." The bedroom was silent for a while as Cassidy allowed Eric to decide between the two options that she had presented him with. "So what will it be?"

Eric sighed. "I guess I'll work for Mr. Thompson."

Cassidy nodded. "Sounds like a good decision." She got up from the bed, the bed squeaking a bit as she lifted her weight from it. "I'll get dinner ready."

"I'm not hungry." Eric's voice was muffled from having his face pressed back into his arms on his knees.

"Well, I'll make some, and if you get hungry later you can come get some." Cassidy left the room and closed the door. She hadn't talked to Dylan about the possibility of having Eric work for him. There was every possibility that he wouldn't want the kid hanging around the store, but maybe he could help her find something for him to do. She sighed. Raising Eric was hard. She hoped that she was doing it right.

The Rumors

Dylan drove back to the feed store, but his mind was still back on the ranch. He had heard some of the rumors about Golden Creek Ranch's new owner, but he hadn't paid much attention. He was trying to recall what he had heard, but instead all he could come up with was Cassidy's eyes. Somehow he had a feeling that the rumors were all wrong.

When he stepped into the store, Zach immediately approached him. "Well? How did it go?" he asked eagerly.

Dylan shrugged. "I took him home and talked to his mom. She's going to take care of it."

"Who is he?"

Dylan almost hated to reveal who the kid was, but he knew that Zach would never let him go unless he did. "Um, he's the kid from Golden Creek Ranch."

"Figures," Zach muttered. "You're living in a dream world if you think his mom is going to take care of that kid."

"Well, I guess I'm just going to give her the benefit of the doubt right now since I only met her for the first time today. How well do you know her?" Dylan heard the challenge in his voice, but he was tired of the small town rumor mill.

Zach blinked. "I've never – I mean, I've seen her once or twice – I haven't, you know . . ." He trailed off. He looked at his feet for a moment. "I'd better get back to work."

"Good idea." Dylan headed into his office, but his mind was unable to focus on the tasks at hand. He kept thinking about the Golden family and wondering what Cassidy was going to do with Eric. He wondered if she would be able to find a home for the dog – especially since she didn't seem to have many friends in the area.

Thinking about the dog reminded him of what Eric was attempting to steal. They wouldn't have food for Carlie right now, and who knew how long the poor animal had been without something to eat, or what Eric had fed her before his pathetic entry into a life of crime.

He went out to the floor, grabbed a bag of dog food that he knew to be good for border collies and headed back to his office. He made a notation on a sheet, and then hollered to Zach that he was leaving early today. He tried to ignore Zach's look of surprise, but knew he was acting strangely.

He got back in his truck, and then decided to make a detour on the way back out to the ranch. Pulling in front of the house he grew up in, he got out and bounded up the porch steps. He rapped on the door, and it wasn't long before Jean answered. She smiled at her son, but her gaze questioned him. He was aware once again that he was not acting as he normally would.

"I have an errand to run, and I would like your company," he said quickly.

Jean nodded. "Okay, just let me grab my jacket." He had a feeling that the response was how one might reply to a person who had suddenly gone crazy, and that they suspected may be dangerous. Jean put on her coat, grabbed her purse and started to go out the door.

"Wait!" She pulled up abruptly and stared at her son. He knew his mom was wondering if the stress had finally got to him and he was having a nervous breakdown. "Do you have paper and a pen or pencil?"

Jean nodded and motioned for Dylan to come inside. She led him to the kitchen table and set a pad of paper and pen in front of him. Dylan quickly scrawled a note and started to get up, but his mom placed a firm hand on his shoulder and then sat down beside him.

"Dylan, I'm not leaving until you tell me what's going on," she said forcefully. "You've been acting strange since you got here, and I have to admit that I'm concerned about you."

Dylan tried to laugh, but the sound that came out only seemed to worry his mom more. He took a breath and decided that he needed to soothe his mom's mind before he took her with him. He explained what had happened after he had gone back to work and of his trip to Golden Creek Ranch. He told her about his thoughts when he had gotten back to work, and then added, "So I decided that I needed to bring them some dog food – for Carlie's sake – and I wanted to take you with me because I think you probably know more about the Goldens than I do. I thought you could clue me in on what the rumors are and what you know to be true."

Jean was silent for a moment as she processed this. "I just would like to know one thing. Do you find Ms. Golden attractive?"

Dylan frowned. "I don't know. I guess she is." He hesitated as he tried to remember what she looked like. "She seems – I don't know – tired, or lonely. Maybe both."

Jean nodded. "Let's go." Dylan looked at her in surprise, but jumped to his feet and grabbed the note. He handed it to his mom after she had gotten settled in his truck. He knew that she read it, but she didn't say anything.

They drove for a while in silence before Jean chuckled.

"I have to admit that you had me worried when you first showed up. I had just bought my plane ticket for Christmas, and I was wondering if I should see if I could return it."

Dylan laughed. "Your expression told me that you wondered if I should be committed to the mental hospital. I suppose I was not quite myself."

"Not at all!" Jean exclaimed. "You've always been calm and collected about everything, even when your father passed away." Her voice shook a bit, but she cleared her throat and continued. "Then you show up at my door looking disheveled and nearly frantic."

"I wasn't frantic!" Dylan protested.

Jean laughed. "Well, you were definitely behaving oddly." Jean shifted slightly in the car seat and turned to watch her son's face. "Now, what would you like to know?"

"The new owner of the ranch is Ray Golden's granddaughter, right?" He waited for his mom's nod. "Why did the ranch go to her?"

"Ray and Nora had one son. Nora once told me that their son was their miracle child because they had been told they wouldn't have any children. His name was Richard, and I think they probably spoiled him." Jean paused a moment trying to remember. "One day, Richard and Ray got in a horrible fight. I don't know what it was about. There were plenty of theories, but no one knew for sure, and Ray never spoke of it. Nora had already passed away by that time – thankfully! It would have broken her heart to see their only child leave and never come home."

"Where did he go?" Dylan took his focus off of the road for a moment to look at his mom. He was glad that she had actually met and talked to the family so she could tell him some of the history.

Jean shrugged. "No one really knows. If Ray did, he

never said."

"Did Ray know about his granddaughter? Before she came back, I mean."

"He did. He once told me about her. I think once she was born, Richard contacted his dad to let him know he was a grandfather. Ray said that periodically, he'd get a picture or note in the mail about her. But Richard was never very good at keeping in touch so they were few and far between." Jean smiled up at Dylan. "I remember that I had seen one of those pictures and had asked who she was, which was the reason Ray told me about her. Ray's eyes lit up when he spoke of her."

"Did they ever come visit?" Dylan tried to think back to what he knew of Ray, but the older man had kept to himself most of the time.

Jean thought for a moment. "Not that I ever remember."

"What happened to Richard?"

Jean shook her head. "I don't know. You'll have to ask someone else."

Dylan pulled his truck into the gravel driveway for the second time that day. "This will only take me a second," he said, as he put the truck in park. He grabbed the bag of dog food and his note and jumped out of the truck. He ran up the porch steps and placed the bag in front of the door. He heard the doorbell ring inside as he pressed the button, but didn't stick around to see if anyone answered. Carlie's barking let him know that Cassidy had allowed the dog inside the house for the time being. He dashed back down the steps and into the truck, quickly putting it in gear and driving away.

Jean didn't say anything, but a small smile tugged her lips. Dylan noticed her amusement. "You think my behavior is ridiculous don't you?"

"I think it's interesting." She looked at him out of the

corner of her eyes. "So what else would you like to know?"

Dylan thought for a moment. "I heard that Cassidy returned with Eric shortly before Ray died and that he left everything to her. I know she still has her maiden name. Do you know anything about her situation? What brought her back? Where Eric's dad is?"

Jean looked as if she finally understood, but she shook her head. "I'm afraid I don't know any of the answers." She felt Dylan look at her. "All I can tell you is the gossip around town, and you know that's not very trustworthy."

Dylan nodded and was silent. Then as if he couldn't hold it in any longer, he asked, "What do the rumors say?"

Jean's lips twitched again. "Oh, there are several. One is that Eric is the result of a one night stand. Another is that Cassidy is in hiding from her husband. Still another says that she and her husband are divorced, and he didn't want anything to do with their child. Any of those could be true, or they could all be lies."

"What about how she is as a mother?" Dylan's grip tightened on the steering wheel. Somehow he knew he wouldn't hear anything good.

Jean sighed. "Most say that she's indulgent to a fault. There are some who say that she reminds them of how Ray and Nora treated Richard and that history will repeat itself."

Dylan shook his head. "I don't see it. When she got on Eric today, he had the look of a boy who knows that he's in trouble, and he's going to pay." He thought for a moment back to what he had witnessed earlier that day. "I wish I could know how she handles it."

"You could ask her," Jean stated simply. "In fact, I would say that you should ask her all the questions you've been asking me. She can tell you the truth about the situations."

Dylan nodded, but his stomach felt sick at the prospect

of asking her such personal questions. "I don't believe the rumors," he said suddenly.

Jean smiled slightly. "To be honest, neither do I."

Dylan looked over at her in surprise. "You don't?"

Jean shook her head. "Rumors may have some basis in truth, but they end up twisting it all up." The truck was silent for awhile. "You have made me think though. I haven't really gone out there and welcomed her. When she first came, Ray was ill, and I didn't want to intrude. Then Ray passed away, and I felt like she could use some space, but I've sort of forgotten about her. I could understand her feeling lonely, moving to a small town where everyone thinks badly of you with no family." Jean straightened in her seat. "I think I'll go visit her. It's long overdue."

Dylan smiled warmly at his mom. "I think that's very nice of you."

He pulled up in front of his mom's house. Jean turned to look at her son, indecision warring on her face. Finally, she tightened her lips in resolve. "I think you should know that I suspect that many of the rumors have gotten their start from her foreman."

"Rex Wilson? Why?"

"I'm not sure, but it seems like every time I hear about her from someone, they start with 'Rex says . . .'" Jean placed her hand on Dylan's arm. "Rex may feel that she's unfit to run the ranch or feel like she's unfair to him. Whatever the reason, he appears to be bent on ruining her reputation and making her unwelcome in Snowfall."

Dylan nodded. "Thanks for all your information. You've given me a lot to think about."

"I wish I had more answers for you, but you know who you really need to talk to." Jean looked closely at her son's face. "Just go slowly," she cautioned.

Dylan looked at her questioningly. "Go slowly?"

Understanding dawned on his face. "Oh, you mean don't push her to answer questions that she's uncomfortable with. Or don't make her feel like she's in an interrogation. Yeah, I wouldn't want to do that." Dylan looked thoughtful. "I'll just have to take it easy."

Jean looked at him for a long moment before she patted his hand on the steering wheel and got out of the car. Dylan had a feeling that his mom's warning had a deeper meaning, but he wasn't ready to explore that yet.

The Foreman

Rex came into the small house on Golden Creek Ranch that had been reserved for the foreman since the first members of the Golden family settled in Wyoming. The old bunk house was no longer in use and had been converted into a guest cottage. Yet here he was, in the same house that had been occupied by generations of foremen before him.

It actually was a nice little house. It was one story with white siding and gray shutters. The Golden family had always kept it in good repair and had updated it with plumbing and electricity long before Rex had arrived. The interior was a little out of date, but that was due to the Wilsons not wanting to spend their own money to redecorate. They felt like the Golden family ought to furnish and redo their home occasionally. In fact, they felt that the family owed them – well, everything.

Rex took off his boots in the mud room and headed into the warm house. He looked for his wife, Mae, and found her cooking in the kitchen. He threw himself into a chair at the kitchen table.

Mae glanced over her shoulder at him. "Are you gonna wash up?" She wrinkled her nose. "I can smell the cows on you."

"You can smell the cows on me every day. I work with cows. I probably smell like horse as well," Rex grumbled, but he got up and headed to the bathroom to wash up. Mae was setting dinner on the table when he came back in. "You overcooked the chicken again." Rex poked the meat with his fork.

Mae gave him a withering look. "Then you can cook your own dinners."

Rex sighed and dug into the unappetizing meal. It wouldn't have hurt Mae to learn how to cook. After twenty-seven years of marriage he would have thought that he would be getting better meals. He looked up at his wife. They were both in their fifties now. Mae had blonde hair – well, she dyed her hair blonde. She'd never been a natural blonde. Her eyes were a hard gray and discontentment had placed unattractive lines on her face. However, she still maintained a nice figure, although Rex wasn't sure how she managed it because she never seemed to do anything, except watch television. She took time with her make-up and hair to look nice and she spent a hefty amount of his paycheck on clothing so she was always in style. All in all, he decided she was worth the frustration she caused him every day. He was always proud to take her into town.

As if she had read his mind, Mae whined, "You haven't taken me to town in days, Rex. I'm so bored out here and who knows when the snow will start up, and I'll be trapped in this God forsaken place."

"We don't have the money to go to town," Rex stated simply around a bite of chicken.

Mae sighed. "That's what you always say."

"Because it's always true. If you didn't spend so much, maybe we could go have some fun every once in awhile."

"And you always blame me," Mae said angrily, throwing her fork down. "I'm not the one that bought a new horse this year."

Rex rolled his eyes. "Oh brother. Here we go again," he

muttered. He took a swallow of the beer that he always had with dinner. "My other horse died, Mae. What did you want me to do?"

"You could have asked Ms. Uppity at the big house to get you a new one. It's a work expense."

Rex wadded up his paper napkin and threw it on the table. "I didn't want that city girl picking out my horse." He stood up and went to scrape his dinner into the trash. It was barely edible anyway, but he had quickly lost his appetite.

"You should have just taken the bill to her after you bought it. What would she do?" Mae rose and cleaned her own plate off.

"Refuse to pay it." Rex leaned against the kitchen counter with his arms folded across his chest.

"Or she might have paid it," Mae argued.

Rex sighed. "That's enough, Mae." He pushed off the counter and headed into the living room.

"How about the new truck? That could have been a work expense, too." Mae followed him into the next room.

"I asked her. She said that my old truck had been working perfectly fine and she hadn't approved the expense."

"That old truck was at least five years old!" Mae squealed.

Rex sighed. They had been over this nearly every day since Cassidy had refused to pay for his new truck. Mae seemed to get some weird pleasure from rehashing it over and over again. Sometimes she enjoyed making him feel like a selfish idiot for buying the truck, and sometimes she liked getting upset at Cassidy for refusing to pay for it. "Well, I don't think you'll get much sympathy from her since the SUV she drives around is at least ten years old, if not more." He flipped on the television and found a football game.

27

Mae stood between him and the TV with her hands on her hips, and he knew what was coming next. "She shouldn't even be the owner of this place. You're the one who worked the ranch when old man Golden was still around. Why would you break your back for him for years if you hadn't expected it to come to you when he died? Instead the idiot leaves it to his citified granddaughter who doesn't know the first thing about ranching."

Rex ground his teeth. He had never been so surprised as he was when Cassidy had pulled in with her son. If he had known the old man had family, he would have found someplace else to work. There was no point in him spending time on a place that wasn't going to come to him someday. When he thought of how polite he had been to Ray, how he had tried to impress him, he cringed.

As Rex had gotten to know Cassidy and her history, hope had resurfaced. The girl was a city girl from the tip of her head to the bottom of her feet. There was no way her grandfather would leave the ranch that he had worked his whole life for to her. She'd just run it into the ground. He guessed that Ray would leave a stipulation that Cassidy and her son be taken care of, maybe they would get the foreman house for life, and he could live with that. It would be better if he could convince her to take the guest cottage, but it wouldn't be terrible if she wouldn't take it.

Then the will was read. Rex remembered the fury that had filled him when he found that everything had been left to his granddaughter. He had only left a measly $100,000 in thanks to his foreman. The money had been spent quickly – partially on debt that had already been incurred. Rex couldn't believe that he had worked this ranch only to lose it to a girl.

Rex glared at his wife. "Thanks for bringing that up again. Like I don't realize it every single day when I have to report to her."

Mae sat down next to him on the couch. "You need to do something."

"I've done what I could. The woman doesn't have a shred of reputation in town. I've made Snowfall as unwelcoming as possible. You'd think she'd take the hint and leave." Rex took another swig from his beer.

"She doesn't ever leave the ranch!" Mae nearly hollered at him. "The woman lets you pick up supplies, orders online when she can, and never seems to need entertainment. She probably doesn't even know that the entire town hates her!"

"What do you want me to do, Mae? I can't just up and leave without a job to go to. We wouldn't last a week on what we have in the bank." Rex looked angrily at his wife, but was surprised at the smug look on her face.

"You should get your own ranch," Mae said triumphantly.

Rex looked at her as if he had just realized how stupid she was. "How do you propose I get a ranch? With what money do expect me to do this? I would at least need enough for a down payment."

Mae pulled out a printout of a ranch that was for sale and handed it to him. "This ranch is up for auction and the family is including the livestock so you wouldn't have to get that either."

"Fine. I still don't have money for a down payment."

"No, but you have assets," Mae smiled knowingly.

"I'm not selling my truck," Rex said firmly. "Or my horse!"

"I wasn't thinking of that. You have access to the ranch accounts."

"That's enough, Mae." Rex changed the channel on the TV hoping that Mae would get the hint and shut up.

"Ray never spent anything that wasn't necessary. He must have had a ton of money tucked away somewhere. Who's going to notice if some of it goes missing?" Mae's eyes widened in false innocence.

Rex looked at her in surprise. "I couldn't do that! I could end up in jail!"

Mae blinked. "Not if she doesn't find out."

Rex turned off the TV and faced his wife, prepared to reason with her. "She's going to find out. It's not like we don't have records of these things."

"A little here, a little there – she'd never see it."

Rex cocked his head to one side. "Have you been watching crime stories again?"

Mae flopped back on the couch and folded her arms across her chest. "Fine! I'm only trying to help."

Rex shook his head and then stopped. He knew how the accounting system worked and he did most of the buying and selling for the place. He could sell some things, take a little bit of the profit or tell her that supplies had cost more than they had and keep the extra. "I hate to admit it, but you might be onto something."

Mae smiled at him smugly. "I'm more than just a pretty face."

Rex didn't feel the need to reply to that comment. He'd have to be careful how he did it, but it just might work.

The Decision

Cassidy heard the doorbell ring and started heading for the door. Carlie was barking enough that she didn't even need a doorbell. When she got there though whoever had been there had left. She could see tail lights down the driveway, and she frowned wondering who had been too impatient to wait for her. She noticed Carlie sniffing around by the door and bent over to see what the dog had found. She picked up the bag and realized that someone had brought dog food. No wonder Carlie had been so interested in the package.

She took the bag inside, quickly found a dish, and filled it for Carlie. Who knew when the poor dog had been fed last. Apparently Eric hadn't thought that far in advance when he had agreed to take Carlie in. The dog ate ravenously, making Cassidy more confident than ever in her decision about not letting Eric keep the dog. He just proved to her that he had no idea how to take care of a pet.

A glimmer of white caught her attention, and she bent over to pick it up. The note must have fallen off the bag of food. A quick note was scrawled hastily on it. Thought you would probably need this until you find a new home for the dog. On the house. Dylan

Cassidy smiled softly. She was glad he had thought about the food. In her distraction about what to do with

Eric, she hadn't given any consideration to the fact that Eric had been trying to get dog food for Carlie. Of course, she would pay for the food when she went to talk to Dylan about having Eric work for him. If he didn't let her, then he may as well have allowed Eric to steal it in the first place, and she wasn't about to let that happen.

Cassidy made dinner and wasn't surprised when Eric ended up joining her after all, although he barely said two words throughout the meal. He kept looking at Carlie and sighing. Cassidy struggled not to roll her eyes, knowing he was trying to manipulate her once more. This time he was using emotional techniques, which she had to admit was more effective than his earlier attempts.

After dinner, Eric went back up to his room taking Carlie with him, muttering something about enjoying it while it lasted. Cassidy sighed as she started cleaning up her own dishes and putting the leftover food away. The truth was she wanted to keep Carlie. She just couldn't allow it after what Eric did.

Why was parenting so hard? She wondered if it was easier if you had a loving partner to help with big decisions like this. Unfortunately, she had never experienced that. She knew that a husband wouldn't solve everything, and in some cases it could make it more difficult, but somehow she felt like having someone to discuss it with and advise her would be helpful.

She had a brief vision of Dylan as he had witnessed her interaction with Eric earlier. He had seemed to understand the position she was in. If he had stuck around longer, she may have ended up asking him what he would do. But he hadn't. Who could blame him? She was a single mom with a thief for a child – at least that was what he had seen.

She closed her eyes and could see Dylan's light brown hair - a little long, curling out from under his cowboy hat.

His face wasn't handsome, but he had a nice face, one that looked like he could be depended on. His hazel eyes, warm smile, and broad shoulders gave him an appearance of strength, someone to lean on. Cassidy shook her head, pushing the image out of her mind. She had enough to keep her mind on without thinking about the feed store owner. What she really wished was that her grandpa or parents were still alive. They would have had advice for her. She may not have always agreed with them, but they definitely would have had advice.

Cassidy mounted the stairs and lightly tapped on Eric's door before opening it. He was lying next to Carlie with his arm thrown around the collie's body. She leaned on the door jamb. "You should take Carlie outside one more time before bed," she said softly, hating to intrude on the moment.

Eric got up slowly. "Come on, Carlie. Let's go outside." He spoke with such an air of gloom that Cassidy felt her lips twitch in spite of herself. He dragged his feet as he led the dog down the stairs and outside. Cassidy stayed at the door of her son's room, a million thoughts flooding her mind. Should she allow Carlie to sleep in Eric's room for the night? What if she couldn't find someone else to take the border collie? Would Dylan agree to her plan? Most of all, was she raising Eric right?

She heard footsteps coming back up the stairs and pulled her mind back to the present. Eric shuffled past her without looking up, but Carlie stopped by her side and licked her hand before following the boy into his room. "Carlie can sleep with you tonight," Cassidy told her son. His head snapped up and a smile lit his face. Cassidy held up a hand. "I'm still going to try to find a new home for her, but while she's here, she can stay with you."

Eric's smile faded. "It's not fair," he grumbled. He

33

started to move past his mom to get ready for bed, but she grabbed his arm.

"Eric, you are trying my patience. You have to see that what you did was wrong, and because of that, I have to discipline you. This is all your own doing, and if you complain about it anymore, I'm not going to let you anywhere near Carlie while she's still here, got it?"

A tear slipped down Eric's face, but he nodded. "I'm sorry, Mom," he whispered.

"I forgive you. Now, get ready for bed." In a short time, a subdued Eric was in bed. Cassidy kissed her son good night, thankful that he still allowed her to do so. Carlie curled up beside the boy's bed and heaved a huge sigh. Cassidy patted her head and headed to her own bedroom. She closed the door and went to sit on her bed. The room had been the guest room while her grandpa had been alive. She couldn't bear to move into his room. The bed was antique and matched the dresser. It was covered in a quilt that her grandmother had made. The walls had peeling floral wallpaper and the floor was covered in a neutral carpet. The curtains had been a darker blue, but were now faded. She knew the room could use updating, but couldn't bring herself to do it since she knew that her grandmother whom she had never met had planned this room. Ray had left it the way it was in her honor, and Cassidy followed his footsteps.

As she looked around, she wondered what her grandma and grandpa would say about the way she was raising Eric. She could almost hear Ray's gruff voice saying, "Get the boy in church! He needs to hear the Word! He needs Christian friends!"

Cassidy frowned slightly. While Ray had been healthy, she and Eric had gone to church with him on occasion. Maybe it was because it was a small town, but she had felt conspicuous and uncomfortable. No one had tried to welcome her or befriend her. So when Ray had gotten sick, it was easy for her to skip going. After he died, it was even easier for her to stop going all together.

She wondered what her son knew of the Bible. His father certainly hadn't taught him what a godly man would look like, and her own teaching was sporadic at best. She wondered if he even knew the basic Bible stories like David and Goliath or Daniel in the lion's den. She groaned and fell back on her bed, only vaguely hearing the squeak it always made. "Oh Father, I have failed. I haven't raised my son the way I should. I doubt if he even knows who You are. Help me to change. Help me to be a better mom. I want him to know You, love You, and serve You, but how will he know if I don't show him?" Tears slipped down her face. "We're going to start reading Your Word together every night. We're going to pray together." She took a deep breath. "And we're going to go to church." With the decision made, she got ready for bed. She had a lot to do in the morning.

The Feed Store

Dylan had the Golden family on his mind all morning.
He wondered if Cassidy had decided what to do with Eric
and if she would follow through. He wondered if she had
found someone to take the dog. He wondered if any of the
rumors about her were true or if they had basis in truth.
Most of all, he wondered why he was thinking about them
so much.

When he had arrived at work, Wayne, his manager, met
him at the door. "I heard we had a little trouble yesterday."
The eagerness in his eyes was apparent. Dylan wondered
how many other people Zach had told. In a small town, it
wouldn't take long for the news to make its way around.
Not that he really blamed Zach. Nothing that exciting
had happened at the feed store as far back as he could
remember. He just felt sorry for Eric if the story had
reached his school. Who knew what the story would have
turned into by the time it got that far? As if he could read
his thoughts, Wayne added, "Did you really tackle the kid?"

"No!" Dylan looked shocked. He had assumed that
Wayne had heard the story from Zach who had seen the
whole thing. "Who told you that?"

Wayne shrugged. "I don't remember, but I heard so
many different versions, it's not surprising that they weren't
all true." Wayne followed Dylan to his office. "So what did

happen?"

Dylan sighed. "The kid came in, took a bag of dog food and tried to leave the store. I followed him and caught him easily – without having to tackle him or harm him at all. I put him in my truck and took him home. That's all."

Wayne looked a little disappointed, but then brightened up. "So what happened when you got him home? It was the Golden kid, right?"

"You sound like a gossiping old woman," Dylan chastised his friend. "Why do you need to know?"

If it had been anyone but Wayne, Dylan would have described his expression as a pout. Wayne was heavy set, middle aged and had a thick beard. His facial expression made Dylan's mouth twitch, but it only partially lessened his irritation.

"Come on, Dylan! It's the most exciting thing that's happened in this town since Grady Keller got caught with a meth lab in his basement."

"That was only two months ago," Dylan reminded him as he took his seat behind his desk.

Wayne leaned against the door. "You may not want to tell me what happened, but that won't stop the town from talking about it. It might be nice to have someone who knows the truth to counteract all the lies that are sure to spread like wildfire." With that Wayne headed back out onto the floor of the store.

Dylan tapped his fingers on his desk for a minute before following Wayne. "What are they saying?"

Wayne grinned. "Who's the gossiping old woman now?"

"Fine. I'm a gossiping old woman. What are they saying?" Dylan wanted to know what rumors were already starting.

"I don't know if I should say." Wayne grabbed a cloth

and began wiping the counter more thoroughly than Dylan was sure it had been cleaned in years.

Dylan folded his arms over his chest. "You know you want to tell me."

"Why do you want to know?" Wayne glanced at Dylan out of the corner of his eye, completely enjoying how the tables had turned.

Dylan placed his hands on the counter. "All right. I went out to the ranch. I met Cassidy Golden and found out that her son had gone behind her back and taken a dog, because she wouldn't let him have one. Because he couldn't tell her about it, and he didn't have any money, he tried to steal dog food for the dog. Cassidy was upset and told him that he wasn't going to keep the dog since he had gotten it behind her back and that there would be more to come. Then she sent him to his room." Dylan took a deep breath. "Now, what are they saying?"

Wayne had leaned forward eager to absorb all that Dylan had to share, but now he leaned back and settled in, relishing his role as news-bearer. "I heard that she met you with a rifle and threatened to shoot if you didn't get off her property. I also heard that she called you a liar for accusing her precious son of doing anything wrong. Another story says that she just laughed when you told her what her son had done." Wayne looked at Dylan intently. "Do you think she'll go through with it?"

"With what? Disciplining her son?" Dylan thought about it. "I'd be more surprised if she didn't. She was really unhappy with her son." He looked up at Wayne. "Do you know the Goldens?"

Wayne shrugged. "I knew Ray and Nora. I can't say I know the new owners of the ranch. Why?"

"Where did all the rumors about them start? Everyone was friendly with Ray and yet no one can stand the granddaughter, but when I went out there, she seemed like a normal single mom. I'm thinking that most, if not all, of the rumors are flat out lies, but who started them?"

Wayne shrugged again. "Where does any rumor start?"

"Why won't anyone in this town get to know the family before they pass judgment on them?" Dylan was muttering more to himself, but Wayne still answered.

"It's not like they've made it easy for anyone to get to know them. When's the last time you saw them in town? They don't go to church or any of the town events that I know of. Kind of hard to get to know someone who seems content to live in isolation." The bell over the door rang, and Wayne stepped from behind the counter to greet the rancher that walked in and help him get his order in.

Dylan returned to his office, but his mind wasn't on his work. Why did Cassidy stay out on the ranch? Why didn't she attempt to dispel the rumors? Was she unaware of them? Or was there some truth to them? Dylan ran his fingers through his hair in frustration. He had to stop thinking about that family! He was done with them.

For quite some time, he was actually able to put the Golden family out of his mind and concentrate on his work. He stepped back out on the floor a little after noon to let Wayne know he was going to take his lunch break. The store was never packed, but the recent events had made the store a place of interest, and several men and women just happened to be there on some business or other, but Dylan knew they were mostly there to hear what had happened and share the rumors they had heard.

Dylan felt his stomach turn knowing that the gossipers didn't care about the truth. They only cared about having a juicy tidbit to share with the next person they saw. He finally found Wayne helping a rancher who had true business to attend to and started heading in his direction.

That's when the bell over the door rang, and silence settled over the entire store. A blast of cold air rushed in, and a woman with her chestnut hair pulled back into a French braid walked in. She wore jeans that fit her slender build, boots, and a plaid shirt covered by a leather jacket.

A group of women near the door distinctly turned their backs on the newcomer and walked away, noses in the air. Several of the men were obviously leering at her. A group in a corner began whispering together. The young woman took a hesitant step forward, and Dylan realized that he'd been staring at her, too. He hurried over to her.

"Cassidy! What can I do for you?" He hoped that she hadn't noticed the welcome she had received, but didn't know how she could have missed it. She had looked relieved when he came towards her.

"Mr. Thompson, I'd like to talk with you, if you have a free moment." She looked around the store, her eyes filling with confusion and hurt. Dylan felt an overwhelming desire to protect her.

"Sure. I was just going on my break. Why don't you come back to my office?" He led the way to the back of the store and gestured to one of the chairs in front of the desk. She took off her coat and sat at the edge of the seat, her eyes going over every inch of the office. Dylan would normally leave the door open with a woman in his office, but knowing that every person in the store would suddenly find an urgent reason to be near his door in order to listen in on their conversation, he shut it. He remained at the door for a moment, his own eyes looking at the office that had been occupied by Thompsons for generations.

There was a large wooden desk in the center cluttered with papers, catalogs and a computer. Pictures of the store lined the walls from the very first Thompson who opened the store to Dylan standing beside his dad. There were a few news clippings on the wall, a bulletin board, a clock, but no windows.

Cassidy smiled nervously. "I like the history of this place." She nodded at the first photograph. "You must be proud of your family heritage."

"Sure," Dylan said quickly. "But you've got a pretty good heritage yourself out there on the ranch."

Her face brightened. "Yes, I do." She straightened in her chair. She had to look awkwardly over her shoulder as Dylan was still standing at the door behind her. "Mr. Thompson," she began, but Dylan held up a finger.

He opened the door, and while he hadn't been surprised to have someone nearly topple into the office, it was obvious by the way Cassidy jumped that it had been unexpected to her. As Dylan had suspected, nearly everyone in the store had found their way to the office door and had been quietly listening. The group sheepishly dispersed with just a look from Dylan. He noticed his own employee slinking away as well. "Really, Wayne? You, too?"

Wayne smiled awkwardly and went back to the register in the front of the store. Satisfied that everyone would now be too embarrassed to listen in, Dylan closed the door and sat in the old wooden desk chair behind the desk. He heard it creak as he sat down and remembered all the times he had heard that same creak when the office had belonged to his father and even his grandfather. "I would keep your voice low, but you should be able to speak with some amount of privacy now." Dylan leaned his arms onto the desk and looked intently at Cassidy. She was still staring in stunned fascination at the door. Slowly she turned to face him.

"Does that happen often?"

"Honestly, no, but the town is sort of buzzing about

the excitement we had yesterday." He knew he had to be completely truthful with her. Maybe she was unaware of the rumors that circled her. She needed to know that she was a target in Snowfall.

Her face flushed. "You mean Eric, I suppose. That's sort of why I'm here." She scooted forward to the edge of her seat. "I told you that I wasn't going to let Eric keep Carlie. I want you to know that I've also grounded him for two weeks – one for lying to me and one for disobeying me. But that still doesn't cover what he did to you."

"Cassidy, you don't have to," Dylan started, but he stopped when Cassidy lifted her hand.

"No, I do. It may not have been much this time, but if he has no consequences for his actions, he may do it again. He needs to learn."

Dylan leaned back in the chair in resignation. "What did you have in mind?"

Cassidy smiled slightly, seemingly grateful that he hadn't argued further. "I want Eric to work for you for the rest of the month without pay. You can have him sweep floors, dust shelves, stock shelves, or wash your truck. I don't care what you have him do, just as long as he's working for you."

Dylan frowned. "The rest of the month seems kind of excessive for what he did."

"I need to know that he'll think twice before doing something like this again. If it's too easy, he may think it's worth the risk." Cassidy's green eyes were pleading with him to understand. Suddenly, Dylan realized that his gut instinct had been right. Cassidy was a good mother. She wanted her son to be a good person. She didn't want to protect him from the consequences of his actions, but she handed them out lovingly.

Dylan nodded slowly. "All right. I'm sure I can keep

him busy."

Cassidy's face lit up as she sprang out of her chair. "Thank you so much!" She grasped his hand and shook it heartily. "He'll be in after school today to talk to you about it, if that's okay with you, but you can start him whenever you want. I don't want you to feel like you have to put him to work today."

Dylan chuckled. "Well, okay then." He had the feeling of being caught in a whirlwind. She headed for the door, but turned back before she had even set her hand on the knob.

"I almost forgot to thank you for the dog food you brought last night," she exclaimed in horror. "I can't believe I didn't start with that."

Dylan stood up. "Don't worry about it."

"No, I want to pay you for it." She reached into her purse, but Dylan stopped her.

"Really, there's no need."

Cassidy looked at him with a look that told him he had missed something. "Eric gets in trouble for stealing a bag of dog food which you later give to us without us paying so we actually did steal the dog food anyway."

Dylan shook his head. "Eric was taking what wasn't his. I am giving you a gift of something I have. It's completely different." Cassidy didn't look convinced. "Look, as soon as you find a home for Carlie, you'll give them the bag of dog food, so think of it as a loan for the next owner."

Cassidy slowly returned her wallet to her purse. "I guess." She didn't sound convinced, but Dylan was glad that she wasn't fighting him on it anymore.

"And, I'm sorry about the whole eavesdropping situation," he added awkwardly.

Cassidy straightened her shoulders. "That's their

problem. Not yours." Her eyes looked sad. "If they wanted the truth, they would have asked. It's not truth they want." She opened the door slowly, and seemed relieved to find that there was no one standing outside. She walked proudly to the door, seemingly oblivious to the stares that accompanied her, but he knew she felt every glance.

Wayne hurried over to his side. "So?"

Dylan looked his employee in the eye. "Mr. Eric Golden is going to be working for us until the end of the month without pay."

"Wait! The thief? You've got to be kidding me!"

"I'm not. Get everything ready. He starts tomorrow." Dylan stepped back into his office and closed the door on Wayne's surprised outburst.

The New Hire

Dylan made sure that he had work to do out on the floor when school let out. He wasn't sure what kind of reception Eric would get, and the store had maintained a steady stream of curious customers all day long. If they had turned their backs on Cassidy, what would they do to the boy who had actually been the one in the wrong?

He saw Eric the minute the door opened. He had jeans and tennis shoes on, and the hood of his jacket was over his head. He scuffed his toes along the ground as he walked and kept his eyes on the floor, shoulders hunched. Dylan wondered how he had been treated at school that day. If he had been teased, shamed, and ridiculed all day long, Dylan figured that it would make him dread coming face to face with him even more. While Dylan had always had good experiences at school, he still remembered how brutal kids could be to other kids. And if their parents were the same people he had been seeing all day, he figured that Eric had been treated cruelly.

Dylan immediately approached Eric before anyone else had taken notice that the boy had entered the store. He wondered if they even knew who he was. "Hey, Eric," Dylan said softly, but with warmth. "Your mom came to talk to me today. Why don't we go into my office?" He led the way and was aware of the murmurs that had started.

Someone must have figured out that the boy who had just walked in was the same one that they had been discussing all day.

Dylan didn't feel the need to check for eavesdroppers this time. Let them listen in. He doubted that there would be anything worth hearing. He dropped into the creaky, wooden chair and faced Eric who was already slumped in his own chair. He had his elbows on his knees and was intently watching the floor. Dylan stayed quiet for a while and just watched the boy. Eric's hair was darker than his mother's – nearly black. It was long enough that it was getting in his eyes. Dylan had noticed the day before that Eric's eyes were the same color green as Cassidy's, sort of an olive green. Eric shuffled his feet against the floor, and Dylan knew he was getting nervous with the silence.

Dylan cleared his throat. "So, your mom's ordering you to do some volunteer work, huh?"

Eric nodded briefly without looking up.

"I can't technically 'hire' you, because you're underage, but I talked with the police and they said that as long as I kept you to just a few hours a day, volunteering wouldn't be a problem."

Eric's head snapped up. His eyes were wide and frightened. "You talked to the police? Why? Why did you have to bring them in on this?"

Dylan held out his hand. "I didn't bring them in on this. I wanted to make sure that I wouldn't get in trouble having you working in the store without getting paid. If that was going to be an issue, I was going to have to work something else out." Eric relaxed, but Dylan could see that his hands were still clenched tightly around the arms of the chair. "If you come in after school, you can work until five and then you can go home."

Eric nodded again. "What kinds of things would I be

doing?"

"Mostly cleaning – sweeping the floors, dusting shelves, cleaning the bathroom, but you may get to stock shelves as well." Dylan paused. "I'm going to need you to be polite to customers." Eric nodded in understanding, but Dylan continued. "I mean, you'll need to be polite, even if they aren't."

Eric met Dylan's eyes. "They don't like my family much around here, do they?" Eric's gaze implored Dylan to be honest.

"They liked your grandfather a lot. There have been some rumors spread about your mother that have sort of not helped the town's opinion. I don't know where they came from, but unfortunately. . ." Dylan stopped awkwardly.

"I just made things worse." Eric looked down at his hands which were now tightly clenched in his lap. Dylan's heart broke looking at the young boy. He was heading into such a trying stage, and he was starting off rough. Eric looked back up at Dylan. "I never noticed that the town was kind of cold to us until today. I had enough friends at school, and I've never minded not being in the popular crowd. I started hearing what people were saying about me – about my mom – today." Eric's eyes began to fill with tears. "When I asked my friends about the rumors, they were surprised that I didn't already know or that I hadn't noticed that we were sort of – I don't know – outcasts or something."

"I'm so sorry." Dylan felt completely inadequate to deal with this situation. "Were they – I mean, today was it . . ." He didn't know how to ask the question, but Eric seemed to know what he was trying to say.

"They weren't very nice to me today, but I guess I sort of deserved it." Eric shrugged. "At least my friends had my back."

Dylan nodded. "Good friends are important. I'm glad they stood with you." He got up and opened a closet. He pulled out a polo shirt. It was royal blue with 'Thompson's Feed' embroidered around a horseshoe in white thread. "You can wear this while you're working for me. You can wear jeans with it. I'm going to go grab a form real quick. I'll be right back."

When Dylan returned he found Eric standing by the wall with the photographs on it. Eric had heard Dylan return so without turning around he pointed at a Labrador in one of the pictures. "Who's this?"

Dylan smiled. "That was Dusty. He was our store mascot." He pointed to another picture where there was a cocker spaniel sitting by the front door. "This was Suzy. She was another mascot."

Eric looked up at Dylan with his eyes shining. "Do you have a mascot now? I could take care of it!"

Dylan shook his head. "Sorry, we haven't had one since before my dad passed away."

Eric wilted. "Why not?"

Dylan shrugged. "Well, at first I guess I was so busy with the store and helping my mom that I didn't have time for one, and I just haven't thought about it much since."

"I've always wanted a dog, but I've never been allowed to have one." He looked wistfully at the photographs once again.

"Why haven't you had a dog?" Dylan went back to his desk chair and sat down. He placed the paper he had brought in on the desk and folded his hands on top of it.

Eric shrugged. "We used to live in this tiny, dirty apartment in the city, and Mom said that it wasn't a good place for dogs. We didn't have much money either, and she said that we couldn't afford to take care of one. Then when we moved out here Mom was busy with Great Grandpa

Ray for a while, and then she was too sad. I think I was wearing her down, but I guess I blew it big time." His shoulders slumped again, and he headed back to sit across from Dylan.

"It probably wasn't the best idea you've ever had." Dylan pushed the paper across the desk and gave Eric a pen. "Fill this out. It's mostly emergency information. If you need to get some of the information from your mom, you can use the phone or you could take it home and bring it back tomorrow if that would be easier."

Eric glanced over the form. "I think I'll take it home, if that's okay."

"That would be fine." Eric stood up, and Dylan walked him to the door. "Do you need a lift home?"

"No. My friend's dad is waiting to take me home. He lives at the ranch right next to ours." He headed out the front door, and Dylan watched him get in an old truck that had seen many years of active duty. Dylan recognized Warren Clifford from church and waved to him. He went back inside feeling secure that Eric was in good hands.

He entered his office and stared at the photographs on the wall. He hadn't realized how many of them had dogs in them. Some of the earliest photos had dogs in them. Dylan thought for a moment. He hadn't realized how much he'd missed the sound of a dog padding around the store. He smiled slowly. It was time for the store to have a mascot, and he knew just which dog he was going to get.

The Mascot

Dylan phoned his mom when he got home. Jean hated text messaging, and often she would purposefully not answer his texts just to get him to call.

"Hey, Mom. Do you remember Dusty?" He could barely suppress his excitement.

"That old lab we used to have? Sure. He tore up your baby blanket that your grandmother had knitted." Jean's tone was dry, but he could hear the humor in her voice.

"That's the one." Dylan chuckled. "I think the store needs another mascot."

Jean paused. "Are you sure, Dylan? A dog is a lot of work. There's a lot of responsibility in having an animal to care for."

"Mom, I'm a grown man. I have the responsibility of the family business to care for every day. I think I can manage a dog." Dylan found himself pacing his living room. He was too excited to sit down.

Jean laughed. "Of course, honey. I sometimes feel like you're still a teenager. Do you have a specific dog in mind?"

"The Goldens' dog, Carlie." Dylan couldn't believe he hadn't thought of it sooner.

"The dog that the Golden boy stole dog food from you for?" She sounded skeptical.

"He attempted to steal it, and he's making up for it. Carlie is a friendly, well behaved dog. She's a beautiful border collie. I think she'll be great for the store."

"Well, it's really your store, so you can do what you want." Dylan sensed a hesitance in his mom.

"Okay, Mom, what is it?" He sat down in his leather recliner and pushed the footrest up. He wanted to be comfortable.

"Oh, I don't know. It just seems like in two days you've become very involved with this family, and I'm not sure that it's the best thing for you."

"What do you mean, 'involved'?" Dylan couldn't believe what he was hearing.

"Well, last night you come over here, talking crazy and dragging me out so that you can deliver a bag of dog food. You asked all sorts of questions about the family." Jean hesitated. "And of course today you got a visit at the store from both the mom and the boy."

Dylan groaned and closed his eyes. "Really, Mom? You're believing the rumor mill?"

"Then they didn't come to the store today?" Jean sounded skeptical.

Dylan was silent. "Well, yes they came to the store."

"Mm. I thought so." His mom sounded like she had won a major point in her argument. "And did you close the door to speak with the woman?"

Dylan burst out laughing. "Is that what this is about? Mom, if you had seen the way the people of this town treated Ms. Golden, it would have made your blood boil. She walked into the store and immediately everyone quits talking. People turned their backs on her. It was ridiculous. She needed to talk to me, and I knew that with the way people had started whispering that they were adding to the gossip. I wanted her to be able to talk in private without half the town listening in." Dylan laughed shortly. "I had some of them about fall into my office when I opened the door suddenly to see if they were eavesdropping. Honestly! Full grown men listening at doors for a juicy piece of gossip to share." Even now, Dylan felt his stomach clench remembering how everyone had treated Cassidy.

"Did she notice?" Jean asked quietly.

"Of course she noticed. It wasn't like they were subtle about it."

Jean sighed. Dylan knew his mom hated to see anyone hurting. "That must have been terrible. So what did she come to talk to you about?"

Dylan flipped in the footrest and leaned forward. "She thanked me for the dog food, told me the punishment that she had given her son, and asked me to help with a part of it."

"I don't see what you have to do with punishing her child." Jean sounded affronted at the idea.

"She figured that since Eric's 'crime' was against me and my store, that he should make some restitution. She asked that he work at the store after school for the rest of the month."

"What did you say?" He swore he heard her mutter under her breath, "like I need to ask."

"I said that I thought it would work." There was silence on the phone for quite a while. Dylan began to feel uncomfortable. "Eric's not a bad kid. He just made a bad decision."

"I just hope you're not inviting trouble to the store." Jean was worried.

"All I want is to do is what I feel like the Lord wants me to do. I feel like this family has been misjudged and badly treated since they arrived, and it's time somebody showed them that they are cared about. I think Cassidy is doing the right thing with the way she's disciplining Eric, and I want to help her." Dylan stared at a stain in the carpet while he waited for his mom to digest this information.

"And taking the dog is something that the Lord wants you to do?"

Dylan smiled broadly. "I sure hope so, because I haven't felt this excited about a decision since I went to college."

"I pray you're not making a mistake about this family. Sometimes rumors are based on truths."

"More often than not, they're more lies than truth. I'm confident about this." He paused thinking his next words through carefully. "You may feel more confident yourself if you got to know them a little bit." He tried not to make it sound like a reprimand, but he knew that in a way he was getting on his mom a bit for judging them before meeting them.

"You're probably right," his mom finally answered after what felt like an eternity. "I should go be neighborly and get to know them a bit better."

Dylan smiled. "I think you would worry a lot less if you did."

*****

The next day, Dylan told Wayne that he'd be in late and headed out to Golden Creek Ranch. He was looking forward to telling Cassidy that he would take Carlie. He knew she was worried about finding the dog a good home. He liked that Eric could still see the dog every day while he worked at the feed store. It would be a good motivator for the boy to do well. He'd make sure to give Eric some chores that involved taking care of Carlie so that he could prove to his mom that he was responsible enough for a dog. He wondered if Eric's heart was too attached to Carlie to accept just any old dog though.

Dylan had been at the ranch often enough when Ray was the owner that he instinctively drove around to the back of the house where there was a door that led straight to the ranch's office. Ray had told him that Nora got so tired of people coming to see Ray and tracking through the house that she had asked him to put a door from the outside to the room so that they would quit interrupting her. Knowing how Ray was well loved and respected, he wasn't surprised that people came to see him often for his advice, or just a cup of coffee.

He rapped lightly on the door and then stuck his head inside. He looked around, but didn't see Cassidy anywhere. He noticed that she hadn't changed anything from when her grandfather had been the one sitting at the desk. Bookshelves lined one wall filled with books on cows, horses, ranching, agriculture, as well as works of fiction – mostly classics – and books on the history of the American west. The desk was metal and set against a window. An old PC was on the desk as well as papers although they were more organized now than when Ray had been in charge. The desk chair was large and leather. It had been a gift from Nora to Ray and had been a treasured possession. Now the chair was faded and there were places where thick tape was holding it together. He felt as if Ray had just stepped out for a moment. There was even a scent of old coffee lingering in the air.

Dylan hesitated. If Cassidy were outside, he wouldn't have much luck in finding her. She could be out riding her horse, tending the large garden, out in the barn or the henhouse, or having a discussion with Rex, the foreman. If she were in the house, he didn't want to go searching for her in her private quarters. That would be awkward to say the least.

While he was still debating, he heard the sound of Carlie's collar jingling and getting nearer. The door from the house opened, and Cassidy came in carrying a mug of coffee and with the dog at her heels. When she saw Dylan, Cassidy jumped so violently that she splashed the hot coffee down the front of her blouse.

"Ow, ow, ow!" She pulled the blouse away from her skin as fast as she could. Dylan felt terrible.

"I'm sorry. I'm used to visiting when your grandpa was the owner. I'd always just walk right into his office. Are you okay?"

"I'll be fine. I don't get visitors often – like ever, so I was surprised. Let me get changed out of this, and I'll be right back." She set her coffee mug down and dashed back out the way she had come in. Carlie stayed behind and watched Dylan with her head tilted to one side.

"I know. I didn't mean to hurt her or scare her." Carlie tilted her head to the other side. "I'm not very good at this apparently." Carlie came over and leaned against him. He patted her side. "Thanks for forgiving me girl. I wouldn't want to start our relationship off on the wrong foot." Carlie licked his hand, and he laughed. "Glad you seem to like me."

He heard footsteps approaching the door, and he took a step forward. "Again, I'm so sorry."

"No, please. It's fine. I'm fine. Everything's – fine." Cassidy tried to smile, but it didn't really come off. Dylan heard warning bells ringing in his head.

"Everything doesn't seem fine. Are you okay?" He took a step near her, but when she wrapped her arms around her middle and took a step backwards, he stopped.

"It's just work stuff." She moved to the large desk chair and sat down. She seemed swallowed up in the large seat. It made her seem vulnerable, and he felt his protective instincts rising.

He pulled out a folding chair that he knew Ray had kept in a corner for visitors and sat down. "You know talking about it may help. I may not have any answers, but sometimes just getting it out there can help the solution become more obvious."

Cassidy looked at him skeptically. Finally, she sighed. "Okay. Maybe you'll see something I've missed." She tucked her feet up underneath herself and settled into her chair. "I've been making some changes to the ranch. I've decided that with me as the owner the place would be better as a guest ranch than a working ranch. I had talked it over with my grandpa before he died - actually he was the one that suggested it. But Rex is being difficult to say the least."

"How so?"

"Oh, he fights me on everything, but today he was eager to sell off some machinery that's been sitting in the barn. Yesterday he sold a tractor, but the numbers didn't seem right. I want to sell some of these things. I need the money from them to finance the renovations, but I want to get a fair price out of it."

"Well, that makes sense. Have you talked to Rex about it?"

Cassidy sighed and shifted slightly in her chair. "No. I don't want him to think that I'm interfering."

"Who's in charge? You or Rex?"

Cassidy chuckled. "Well, it should be me, much to Rex's chagrin. He doesn't think a 'city girl' like me can handle this job."

"Seems like you've done okay," Dylan observed. "You've been here a few years, and the ranch seems to be thriving under your leadership."

Cassidy glowed under the praise, and he realized that she was really all alone in this venture. Eric was too young to support her, although he supposed that Eric had his share of chores around the ranch. Rex was certainly not going to encourage her, and Mae wasn't really the type to befriend another woman. With the isolated life she had lived on the ranch since her grandfather's death, she had borne the burden without any support, encouragement or help.

Dylan cleared his throat awkwardly. "I actually came to tell you that I think I found someone to take Carlie." The dog's head perked up when she heard her name.

"Really?" Cassidy smiled broadly. "Who?"

"Me." Dylan looked at her boyishly.

"You?" She narrowed her eyes. "Are you just taking her out of pity? Was there really no one else to take her?"

"No and no. Actually Eric noticed some of the pictures on the wall of my office had dogs in them, and I remembered that the store used to have 'mascots' back in my grandpa's day and even my father's. There were even dogs in some of the really early pictures. I thought that it was about time the store had another mascot, and Carlie seemed like she would be a perfect fit." Carlie thumped her tail against the floor.

Cassidy looked over at Carlie and called her name. The dog immediately came over to Cassidy's side. Cassidy took the dog's face in her hands. "You would be a good dog for Mr. Thompson, wouldn't you?" The dog licked her chin. "She really is a nice dog. She's well trained and even tempered. I wish that Eric had just asked me, because I would love to keep her." She looked over at Dylan. "But Eric would be happy that he could see her every day at the store." Her face shadowed. "Could we keep her one more night? She's been sleeping in Eric's room, and I'd like to give him a little warning."

"That would be just fine. I can come get her after Eric goes to school tomorrow, and Carlie will be waiting for him at the store when he gets off of school."

Cassidy smiled. "That sounds perfect." She stood up. "Thank you so much! This seems like a perfect solution." Her eyes twinkled. "You may find that even after your deal with Eric is over that he still haunts the feed store."

"He'd be more than welcome," Dylan reassured her.

"You say that now, but wait until you've had him with you a few weeks."

The Vet

Cassidy was out riding her horse, Ranger, when the vet came to check on her herd. She saw the dust on the driveway, and was amazed that she could still see the dust in December. Normally, the snow would have covered the ground by now, but this year had been dry. She spurred her horse on towards the house and got there shortly after the vet had stopped her truck.

Dr. Gerri Hutchinson had been the vet for the ranchers near Snowfall for years. Her father had been the vet in the area before her. As Gerri got out of the truck with her equipment, she smiled warmly at Cassidy. It suddenly struck her that Gerri was the closest thing she had to a friend here. She didn't know why she had never felt lonely before. Maybe she had filled her spare time with work and Eric, but with the arrival of Dylan Thompson in her life, she was now keenly aware of how alone she was.

"So what's going on?" Gerri asked, as the two women began walking toward the field where the cattle was kept, Cassidy leading Ranger behind her. Even though no snow had fallen, the days were chilly and the cows were kept warm in a field near the barn.

"I'm turning the ranch into a guest ranch so I'm selling off some of the herd. I don't want to get rid of all of them, but keeping up with such a large number and doing all the work for the guests would be too much. I know it's not the best season for auctions, but Rex took a few of them to auction, and they didn't bring in as much as I expected. When I questioned him about it, he said that the cows he had sold had been sick recently and lost weight."

Cassidy explained the situation and noticed Gerri's confusion immediately. She started to think that her suspicions that Rex wasn't being completely honest about what had happened were true.

"There were no signs of illness when you chose them?" Gerri asked professionally. "That is, I assume you chose them."

"Yes, I did and no, I didn't see any signs of illness. In fact, these were some of the healthiest of the herd. That's what concerns me. Could they have gotten that sick, that fast? If they did, is it something that could spread? I can't afford to have the whole group decimated." Cassidy put her free hand in her jean pocket as they continued to walk and tightened her grip on Ranger's reigns. Something wasn't adding up.

"It does seem strange. I think you made the right decision to call me. I know Rex thinks he can do everyone's job, including my own," Gerri said with a smile. "But if this is true, then we need to figure out what's going on." Cassidy glanced over at Dr. Hutchinson. She suspected that something was off, too. What was it?

They arrived at the field and began checking out the stock. Cassidy looped Ranger's reigns around the fence and followed the doctor inside. Dr. Hutchinson would occasionally ask for Cassidy's assistance, and Cassidy was struck again by the way that Gerri had with animals. It was definitely something that was in her blood. You could tell that she genuinely cared for the well-being of the animals as well as the effect any illness would have on the rancher.

In the distance, Cassidy heard barking. She turned and saw Carlie bounding toward them. Not knowing how the dog was around horses, Cassidy had left her behind when she had gone for a ride. She didn't want the dog to spook the horse or get kicked in the face because she was teasing him. She watched Carlie approach warily, hoping that she wouldn't pester Ranger. The horse was shuffling his feet and his eyes were nervous as he watched the dog approach, but Carlie had no interest in the horse. She stopped at the fence and placed her front paws on the top, tilting her head to one side as if asking for permission to enter.

Dr. Hutchinson laughed. "Well, Carlie, it's good to see you again." She went over and greeted the dog warmly. "I wondered what had happened to you when your family moved. I know they were looking for a home for you, and it looks like you got one."

"Well, it's kind of a long story," Cassidy began as she explained how Carlie had arrived at their ranch. "So, I can't keep her because of what Eric did, but we did find her a new home. She's going to be Thompson's Feed Store's new mascot."

Gerri nodded as she continued to rub Carlie's fur. "I think that would be a good place for her. Lots of people to lavish some attention on her, and Dylan has always had a way with dogs. It's a shame that it didn't work out differently though. She might be good protection for you."

Cassidy stiffened. "Why would I need protection?"

Gerri refused to meet her eye. "Your cattle are perfectly healthy. I can't find anything wrong with them, which makes me concerned about what happened earlier." She finally made eye contact with Cassidy. "I fear that you have an enemy and whoever it is has decided that this would be the best way to hurt you. It may have been simply rumors at the auction, someone trying to get a lower price. Or maybe it's something else."

Cassidy felt her stomach sink. She didn't go to town often, but that hadn't kept the rumors from reaching her. Were they now infiltrating her professional life? "Something else, like what?"

"Hey!" A shout drew both women's attention. They saw Rex striding toward them, anger clearly written on his face and purpose in every stride. He got just inches away from Cassidy, looming over her with a clear intent to intimidate. Cassidy held her ground and stood straight, looking him directly in the eye. She was in charge, and it was time he understood that. "I told you not to call in the vet." He jerked his thumb towards Gerri. It was well known through Snowfall that Rex didn't much care for Dr. Hutchinson. Rex had respected her father, but didn't feel like a woman was capable of doing the job right. Cassidy had been shocked that this sort of feeling was still around in the modern day and age, but it was right in front of her every single day.

"I know you did, and while I respect your opinion, I had some valid concerns about the well being of the herd." Cassidy could see Gerri silently applauding her from behind Rex.

"Leave it to a woman to worry about nothing." Rex spat on the ground, and Cassidy tried hard not to show her disgust. She knew he did it in front of her because it irritated her.

"It's not nothing when we lose money on sick cows that were healthy the day before. It could be a virus that could take out the entire herd. That would be disastrous for both of us."

Rex smirked. "Sure. But I know cows, and I know they're fine."

"You didn't know that the ones you took to auction

weren't fine." Cassidy paused just a moment. "Or did you?" Suspicion suddenly flared. Who hated her more than Rex? He had made it clear that he thought she was inept at best and a mooching gold digger at worst. But how would lowering the price of the cattle benefit him? If she went under it would hurt him as well. She would have to sell everything, and he'd be out of work. What possible profit would he receive from that?

Rex's eyes shifted briefly, but he didn't back down. "My best guess is that they strayed too far from the heat and took sick."

Gerri took a step forward. "I could verify that guess if you'd like. I can look them over."

Rex swung around to face the vet. "They're long gone by now. It was an out of state buyer who got them." A bead of sweat trickled down his face. Cassidy's eyes narrowed. Even without snow, the chill in the air was pronounced. Rex was nervous about something.

"I see," Dr. Hutchinson replied, her tone conveying that she saw more than Rex would like her to see. She turned to Cassidy. "I would keep an extra close eye on the herd, and if anything else suspicious happens, I would call in the sheriff." Rex's face paled.

"You two women take the cake!" His voice growled through his teeth. Carlie growled and got between him and Cassidy, pressing herself against Cassidy's legs. "You jump to conclusions without any evidence. Think there's some sort of conspiracy going on. Let me tell you something." He started towards Cassidy with his finger out, but backed off when Carlie growled again. "Let me tell you something, I know this herd, and you don't. I'm the foreman and you are nothing, but a glorified paper pusher, a city girl who clearly doesn't know the risks involved with ranching." He lowered his voice. "Why don't you just go back to the city?"

Gerri folded her arms across her chest. "I'd be careful of how you threaten Ms. Golden right now, Rex. You may be considered a suspect when the criminal investigation begins." She smiled sweetly. "And I'd be more than happy to testify about what I just heard."

Rex spun on his heal and stormed away, muttering and swearing under his breath.

Cassidy took a deep breath and tried to shake off the tension in her shoulders. "Thank you," she said earnestly.

Gerri placed her arm around Cassidy's shoulders. "Why do you put up with that guy? Let him go! You can do this without him." They started back toward the house. Cassidy left Ranger at the fence, deciding that she would take care of him after she saw the vet off. Carlie bounded happily between the two women.

"In Grandpa's will, he asked that Rex be given a job here for life. The only exceptions were if Rex were to prove himself to be untrustworthy, or if Rex decided to leave of his own will." Cassidy had wondered often how Ray had come to hire Rex, and what had instilled such loyalty towards him.

"So, we'll just have to prove that he's untrustworthy. Shouldn't be too hard to do. I've often suspected that he is the one who started those rumors about you around town." They arrived at Gerri's truck, and Cassidy turned to face her.

"I've been hearing about these rumors, but I've been most aware of them recently. How long have they been going on?" Cassidy tried to hide the hurt she felt, but she knew her eyes betrayed her.

"They've been going around since you arrived." Gerri patted her arm. "Don't worry about it. Once people know you, they'll realize that they're not true."

Cassidy shook her head. "They won't get to know me because of the rumors. In case you haven't noticed, I'm not exactly popular around town."

Gerri placed her hands on her hips. "In case you haven't noticed, you haven't tried very hard to get involved." Gerri's face softened. "Honey, you can't go through life alone, and you are trying so hard to barricade yourself against everyone. You can tell yourself that they won't like you and that it's not your fault because they all believe the rumors, but the truth is, that if you would try, you could set the rumors straight. You're just afraid to go out there." Gerri sighed. "I know that we're not really close, and I probably have no business talking to you like this, but every time I come out here, I leave wanting to shake some sense into you. I think we could be friends, but you block everyone out." She opened her truck door and threw in her bag. "Think about it, okay?"

Cassidy nodded, stunned into silence. She watched the vet drive away and then headed back down to get Ranger.

The Visit

Cassidy was still thinking about the mystery that was enveloping her and Gerri's comments about shutting herself out when she began preparing dinner. Eric wasn't home from his first day working at the feed store. She had told him to call her when he was near the end, and she would come and get him, but she hadn't heard anything. It was dark already, and Cassidy was beginning to wonder if she should just head into town and get him when she saw headlights coming down the driveway. She grabbed a sweater off the hook by the door and wrapped it around herself as she stepped out on the porch.

A sedan pulled up and stopped, but instead of Eric emerging as she had expected, an older woman climbed out. She had grabbed a plate out of the passenger seat and headed up the stairs. She gave a small smile, but there was some sort of strain in it. Cassidy wasn't sure if it was nerves or embarrassment, but the woman seemed reluctant to be there.

"I haven't been very neighborly, I'm afraid," the woman began when she reached the porch. "It would serve me right if you didn't want to see me at all, but I didn't want to bother you when your grandpa was ill, and then I didn't want to intrude on your grief when he died, and, well, I guess time got away from me." She shrugged awkwardly.

"That's completely understandable," Cassidy said gently. She was curious about why this woman had suddenly decided to introduce herself. Had Gerri talked to her? Or had a guilty conscience brought her to the ranch? Or perhaps curiosity about the talk going around town?

"I'm Jean Thompson, Dylan's mom." She thrust the plate into Cassidy's hand. "I made some of my snickerdoodle cookies."

Knowing that she was Dylan's mom at least cleared up why she was there. She was probably concerned with the amount of time Dylan was spending with the town outcasts. "Thank you. I love just about anything with cinnamon." Cassidy glanced down the road with some concern and then smiled at her visitor. "Won't you come inside?" She opened the porch door and allowed the woman to proceed her inside.

Cassidy put the cookies on the table and gestured to a chair inviting Jean to sit. She took the chair opposite, glancing at her phone while trying to hide it, but she was unsuccessful.

"Is this a bad time?" Jean still looked uncomfortable, and Cassidy regretted the impulse that had made her look at the phone.

"No. No, I'm sorry. I just expected my son home by now so I'm a little jumpy. I told him to call when he was ready. . ." Without thinking she glanced at her phone again.

"Your son is working with Dylan, isn't he?" Jean smiled in understanding. A mother relating to another mother.

Cassidy nodded. "His first day was today."

"I'm guessing that Dylan told him that he would bring him home, but he had to close first. I would be surprised if he didn't at least offer." Jean reached across the table as if to pat Cassidy's hand in comfort, but then pulled back.

Cassidy smiled, but it didn't reach her eyes. "That's most likely it." She thought about Jean's action and felt sad. It was as if she could feel the rumors sitting between the two of them. Gerri had felt that Cassidy had helped the rumors spread by keeping herself isolated. At the time it had felt like she was protecting herself and Eric, but maybe she had created an insurmountable barrier between herself and her neighbors. She had a few ranchers who helped her on occasion, including Warren Clifford who had a son Eric's age. She had a feeling that it was due more to their respect for the memory of her grandfather than anything else, but she appreciated their help. Still she always felt a distance. "How many of the rumors do you believe about me?" Cassidy didn't know where the question had come from, but it erupted from her before her mind could censor it. She was embarrassed to feel her eyes filling with tears. She supposed the day had left her feeling emotionally vulnerable.

Jean's eyes widened in surprise, and her face flushed in discomfort. She stammered around for a while. "I don't . . . I just . . . well, it's hard to say . . ." Jean took a deep breath. "I'm sorry." She looked at Cassidy with tears filling her own eyes. "We haven't made your transition here very easy, have we?"

Cassidy felt a tear slip down her cheek. "Dr. Hutchinson was here today, and she thinks I'm partly to blame. I tried to isolate myself from the lies and instead I just confirmed them."

This time Jean didn't second guess her impulse. She laid her hand on top of Cassidy's. "I wouldn't want to face everyone if they thought horrible things about me. I think it's normal to want to protect ourselves from hurt – physical or emotional."

To both women's surprise, Cassidy burst out with a loud, heart-wrenching sob. She placed her head on her arms and cried like an overtired toddler. Jean stood up and went behind Cassidy. She rubbed her back gently and murmured words of encouragement. It was several minutes before Cassidy was composed enough to raise her head. She stood up and grabbed a wad of paper towels to dry her face and blow her nose. Sitting back down, she found that Jean had taken the chair next to hers instead of across the table, and it warmed Cassidy's heart.

"I'm so sorry," Cassidy said, her breath still catching from the exertion of crying so hard and so long.

"I'm guessing that you've needed to let that out for a long time."

Cassidy laughed shakily as she sniffed. "I think you're probably right."

"Wanna talk about it?" Jean asked the question softly, and instinctively Cassidy knew that she wouldn't press if she said no. But with Gerri's words so fresh in her mind, Cassidy knew that it was time that she set some things straight.

"You said that we want to protect ourselves from physical pain, but I didn't." Cassidy's breathing turned shallow as she remembered. "My parents died when I was in college. My dad had learned to pilot, and they had gone in his little plane, but a storm came up faster than he had expected." She sighed sadly. "Anyway, I was a little lost when they died, and I turned to Brad for comfort." She nearly spit the name out in disgust. "Brad was – well, the epitome of the bad boy – motorcycle, leather, long hair, tattoos. Grandpa would not have approved." She chuckled. "Which is probably why I stayed away from here. I didn't want him to tell me that I was ruining my life with Brad, but it would have been the truth." Cassidy looked up at

Jean and saw no judgment, just compassion. "I found out I was pregnant only a few months after my parents were killed. Brad wanted me to – he didn't want the baby, he didn't want me." She shrugged. "But I was scared, and I didn't know what to do. So I pestered him, begged him, promised him anything to get him to marry me so that the baby and I wouldn't be alone. He finally agreed. It wasn't until much later that I realized that when he decided to marry me was when he found that I had received an inheritance from my parents' death."

"I don't think you're the only woman to ever do that. It would have been a very emotional and trying situation." Jean looked at the table for a moment. "Why didn't you come here after your parents died?"

"I was in school. I didn't want to just up and quit. I intended to get my degree, but then I ended up dropping out anyway." Cassidy swallowed. "Brad didn't want me in school so I quit. Well, he didn't want to spend the money on my schooling anyway. We had Eric, and for a few months things were okay – not great, but okay. Then Brad got tired of playing house, and he began to stay out late. I never asked questions about where he was. I didn't want to know the answers. Some nights he'd come home drunk, and we'd fight." She swallowed again, and she started breathing faster.

"Did he hurt you?" Jean's voice was soft, as if she knew the answer, but didn't want to hear it.

Cassidy nodded. "I put up with it – I was afraid to be alone. I told myself that Eric needed a dad in his life." Cassidy started tearing a paper towel into tiny pieces. "One day I left Eric in Brad's care for an hour. I came home to find Eric home alone, and he had a bruise already showing on one side of his face." Cassidy's eyes sparked as she looked up at Jean. "It was one thing for him to hurt me. It was something totally different for him to hurt my son. I wasn't about to put up with that. I called my grandpa, and he told me to come to the ranch right away. Before Brad could come home, I packed a bag. I packed light enough that I hoped that he would think that we just went out for a minute and would be back. Grandpa welcomed us with open arms. He chastised me for not coming to him sooner, but it was done in love. My parents raised me in church, but I never had a relationship with God. At least, not until I moved here. Grandpa took us to church and suddenly everything made sense, and I became a Christian." Cassidy played with the pile of torn up paper on the table. "I heard from a friend not long after I arrived here that Brad had been killed in a motorcycle accident. He had been drinking at the time. It was only then that I breathed easy."

"Did you go back to your maiden name after you left, or had you always kept your name?" Jean asked in curiosity.

"I legally changed my name back after Brad's death. Grandpa helped me. I wanted to put it all behind me."

"Understandable. And now I've brought it all back to the surface." Jean looked contrite.

Cassidy smiled. "" She took a breath. " Anyway, I just needed someone to know the truth. I don't know what has been said, especially about me being a single mom and everything, but maybe if I had a few people to trust with what actually happened, maybe that will eventually start spreading truth instead of the lies."

Headlights swept through the room, and Cassidy bolted to her feet. She wiped her face and ran outside. Dylan and Eric stepped out of the truck. Eric bolted up the steps and called for Carlie.

"Hey!" Cassidy grabbed her son's arm. "Why didn't you call me?"

"Mr. Thompson said that he'd take me home. I figured that was better than you having to come to get me."

"You could have let me know!"

Eric looked more closely at his mom. "Mom, have you been crying? I'm sorry, Mom. I didn't mean to upset you. Please don't cry." He wrapped his mom in a hug.

"I'm fine. I just didn't know where you were." Cassidy squeezed her son.

"You okay now?" Cassidy nodded. "Can I go find Carlie?"

Cassidy laughed. "Sure. Dinner will be ready soon." Eric ran off, eager to find his dog.

Dylan stepped closer. "Were you crying about Eric? I'm sorry we worried you." He looked concerned.

"Not crying about that in particular. Just remembering and got emotional." Cassidy decided it was time to change the subject. "Would you like to stay for dinner? Your mom is here."

"I noticed her car. If it wouldn't be too much trouble I would love to stay." Dylan held the door open for Cassidy.

"I just invited your son to stay for dinner. You're welcome to join us if you'd like," Cassidy told Jean.

"That would be lovely. Can I help?" Cassidy and Jean got to work on dinner while Dylan set the table.

They sat down to eat and enjoyed getting to know one another better. As they were enjoying Jean's cookies, Cassidy decided it was time to bring up the subject of Carlie's new home.

"I found someone to take Carlie today," she began. Eric put his cookie down, his face showing the strain of the news. "I think it will work out well for everyone."

"Who is taking her?" Eric asked softly.

"Actually, it's me," Dylan said. "You gave me the idea when you reminded me of our store mascots. It's high time we had another one. So you'll still get to see her and take care of her every day when you come to the store."

"You're not going to leave her alone at the store at night, are you?" Eric asked anxiously.

"No, she'll come home with me when we close, or stay with me if I'm not working that day. I'll take good care of her, and you can visit her whenever you'd like." Cassidy looked at Dylan sharply at that. She wondered if he knew what he was offering. Eric might be over at his house every single night. "And while we're clearing things up, I'll plan on bringing Eric home every night after he's done with work, if that works for you."

"Yeah, sure, that would be fine." Cassidy was flustered by the help that Dylan seemed so eager to give. It had been a long time since someone had looked after her.

Dylan smiled. "With that settled, let's clean up. You and I will take clean up duty, Eric, since our moms did the cooking."

Without even a murmur, Eric jumped to his feet and started helping. It didn't take long before everything was clean. Dylan assured Cassidy that he had Eric work on his homework while Dylan was closing the store, so she allowed Eric to go play with Carlie. She bid her guests farewell and then leaned against the door. It hadn't been easy, but she felt like maybe she was on her way to having some real friends for the first time in a long time.

******

Dylan stopped his mom before she got in her car. "What was Cassidy crying about before we got here?"

"She decided it might be beneficial to share some truths about her past to counteract the rumors. It was emotional for both of us." Jean patted his arm. "I'll tell you later, but right now, I'm worn out. This visit was a bit more than I expected."

"Okay, but I'm going to hold you to that." Dylan watched his mom climb into her car and drive away. He glanced once more at the house before getting into his truck. He had a feeling that Cassidy had dealt with more than he could imagine. He wondered why he cared so much.

The New Plan

Rex paced the living room ignoring Mae's protests that he was blocking her view of the TV. That city girl had to go and call the vet after he had expressly told her not to. He knew that the vet suspected him, but he also knew that she had no evidence of anything – yet. She didn't know that the cows hadn't been sick. He wondered how much Cassidy suspected. How was he going to get enough for a ranch of his own without raising the alarm?

"Rex! For the last time, get out of the way! I'm gonna miss who the bachelor gives the rose to!" Mae's voice brought him back to the present. He scowled at her, but her eyes were riveted on the screen.

Personally he couldn't stand watching each new pretty boy pick from dozens of beautiful women, although the antics the women went through to get his attention did amuse him. Yeah, must be nice to have women making a fool of themselves over you, willing to do anything to get your attention.

He looked at Mae to find her tearing up with the woman who had to go home. Rex shook his head. The show was finally over. Rex grabbed the remote and turned off the set.

"I can't think with that racket going on," he growled.

Mae jumped to her feet and put her hands on her hips. "You wouldn't put up with me turning the TV off on you!

What makes you think you can do that to me?"

"You watch television all day long. I work all day. I deserve to get to relax when I get home. That's the difference." Rex knew he was taking out his anxieties and frustrations on his wife, but honestly, he didn't care. Mae annoyed him.

"Yeah, I don't work. How do you think this house get cleaned or dinner cooked? Fairies?" Mae folded her arms across her chest.

Rex looked around at the stacks of dishes on the coffee table, the laundry on the couch, and the layer of dust on everything. "Yeah, the house is immaculate. I don't know how you do it," he said with more than a little sarcasm lacing his voice.

"All right, Mr. Smarty Pants, let's see what happens when I don't do anything!"

"It couldn't be any worse than it is now!" Rex was yelling now. "Maybe the mice and roaches will clean it up!"

Mae's eyes teared up. "I do the best I can." She sat down on the end of the couch without laundry on it and began to cry.

Rex rolled his eyes. Mae always pulled that trick when she had no other way out of an argument. And it worked every time. Rex sighed. "I'm sorry, Mae. It's not you. It's that woman!"

Mae's tears instantly dried up. "The city girl? What did she do now?"

"Remember that plan I had to sell things and pocket some of the profit so we can get our own place?"

"Yeah. Did she find out about it?" Mae's eyes widened. Even she knew there were dangers in what Rex was doing. Usually Mae didn't pick up on the risks when Rex had a less than honorable plan. It made Rex realize that this time he was risking more than he ever had before. Mae probably didn't get the full scope of what the consequences could be, but she knew there could be loss. Rex could certainly lose his job, lose his dream, but worse, he could go to jail. He was aware of it. When that vet woman had mentioned bringing in the sheriff he had felt a chill through his entire being.

"She doesn't know everything, but she's suspicious." Rex began pacing again. "I told her not to call in the vet, but she had to go and do it anyway!"

Mae gasped and got to her feet. "She didn't listen to you? What did the vet say?"

"She said the herd is healthy and she would consider the results of the auction suspicious."

"Do they know what happened?"

Rex looked at his wife. "No. They think the cows were sold for too low a price, but they don't know that I have the extra amount." Rex took a deep breath. "What am I going to do, Mae?" He couldn't believe he was asking her opinion. "The money I've skimmed from the profits isn't going to buy us a ranch, but if I take more I'll raise her suspicions and she'll start investigating. If I lay low for a little bit, maybe she'll kind of forget, and then I can start taking more off again."

"I don't know why you had to tell her the price from the auction anyway. How would she ever know?"

Rex put his hands in his pockets. "She'd know. I don't like her, but she knows everything about this ranch. She knows exactly how many cows she has. She knew exactly which ones I was talking about when I told her. She knows what they're worth and what is in each account."

Mae sank back onto the couch and grabbed the remote. Flipping the TV back on, she said, "Seems like you're stuck."

The news was on, and a man in a suit was giving the weather report. Mae went to flip the channel, but Rex stopped her. "I need to know what's coming. I've heard the weather's going to change, and there's talk of a storm."

Mae sighed and rolled her eyes. "Fine." She tossed the remote onto the coffee table and slumped back in the couch.

As the weatherman went on about the storm, Rex had a thought. There was a storm coming. It was going to be rough. He was going to have to get the cows in a safe place. Cassidy would be holed up in the office or the house, not wanting to brave the storm. What better time for him and Mae to disappear? They could take the entire herd with them. He was sure he could get a loan for a small spread if he already had the livestock. By the time the storm broke, and she was able to leave her house, the cows would be sold, and they would be across state lines with the money. Maybe they'd even head into Canada and buy a ranch up there.

"I know what we're going to do, Mae," Rex said quietly. "But I'm going to need you to start packing."

The Church

"Time for bed, Eric." Cassidy stuck her head in her son's room. With being grounded, it wasn't surprising that she found him reading. All electronics were forbidden during grounding which didn't leave much for Eric to do. He did enjoy reading, however. He'd been enjoying mostly old westerns by Zane Grey or Louis L'Amour since they had moved to the ranch. She sometimes thought that he wished their lives were more like those stories, filled with rustlers, shootouts, and long cattle drives. The modernity had stolen some of the romance of ranching away – though it definitely made the day to day chores easier.

"Ah, Mom! It's Saturday." Eric put his book down, but left his finger in place. She knew he was hoping that she would relent.

"I know, but we're going to church tomorrow." Even as she said it, Cassidy's heart sped up. She was keeping her promise to God, but it scared her to no end.

Eric sat straight up. "To church? We haven't been to church since Grandpa Golden died."

"I think it's time for us to go back. I want you to have a better foundation for life than I've been giving you." Cassidy paused and looked at the toes of her socks. "To be honest, I need a better foundation in my own life. I used grief as an excuse to allow it to crumble, but it's time to get my life back on track."

She glanced up to find Eric staring at her as if he had just discovered that she was an alien. "Okay," he said slowly. "So, how long are we going to do this? Through Christmas? Easter? Then we'll go back to normal?"

Cassidy frowned. She couldn't believe she had allowed both of them to get to this point. "No. This is going to be our new normal. It's time."

Eric studied his mom. "Is this part of my punishment?"

Cassidy had to chuckle. "No, this is what I should have been doing all along."

Eric looked unconvinced. "Okay." He set his book down and started his nighttime routine. After putting him to bed, Cassidy went back downstairs. She sat on the couch near her grandfather's old recliner.

"I know this is the right thing to do, Lord. So why am I so scared?" Cassidy leaned her head back against the couch and closed her eyes. "I've been away so long. It's hard to break old habits. I'm scared that they won't accept me. I'm scared that they'll believe the lies. I'm scared it'll be too hard, and I'll fail again. Most of all, I'm scared that it's too late for Eric, that I've cemented him in bad habits, and that his foundation has already been laid."

She thought about how she had taken Eric to church as a baby, but Brad had ridiculed her for it. Eventually, he had told her that if she wanted to be brainwashed, it was fine, but she had to leave Eric behind. So she stopped going altogether. When she had moved to the ranch, her grandpa had required that they attend church. In her grief over losing her grandpa, she had stopped going.

She sat up. When her parents had died, she had turned from the support of the church family and into the reluctant arms of Brad. When her grandpa had died, she had once again turned from church to wallow in her grief at home, isolated and alone. Why did she turn from God in her pain instead of towards Him?

She thought back to her parent's accident. She had been legally an adult, but felt like a kid. She had been given not only all her parents owned, but their life insurance as well. When Brad had used nearly all of it to pay his debts, she had recognized why he had suddenly changed his mind about marrying her.

She remembered feeling lost and alone. The people in her church had tried to comfort her, but some of their well-meaning words had hurt.

They're in a better place now. Sure, but she was in the worst place of her life.

God has a plan. If this was God's plan, she wasn't sure she wanted any part of Him..

God is always with you. Well, it sure didn't feel like it.

God never gives us more than we can handle. He must have a high opinion of how strong she was, because it sure felt like more than she was able to cope with.

God loves you. If He loved her so much, why would He take both of her parents away from her?

After the funeral, the church family had seemed content with their platitudes and vague offers to help – let me know if you need anything. She wanted to scream, "I need my parents back!" What good would it have done? No one had checked on her, no one had called, no one had come alongside her. She was alone. She felt abandoned – not by her parents, not even the church, but by God Himself.

So she turned to Brad. The biggest mistake of her life. The only positive of that relationship was Eric. He had given her life a purpose.

When she finally had come to Golden Creek Ranch, she had felt like she belonged again for the first time in a very long time. She had loved that last little bit with her grandfather. He had hated when she had to care for him, but she had done it joyfully. She was safe, she was loved, and she was home.

Then he had passed away, too. And she heard the same platitudes all over again, the same insincere offers, with the same outcome. No one really cared about her. God didn't really care about her. So she left the church again. But she had learned not to fill the void with another scumbag like Brad. Instead she learned to ignore the emptiness.

Maybe she just didn't get it. Maybe she didn't understand who God was or what He was doing in her life. Yes, some of her problems were caused by her own bad choices, but some things were out of her control. She really didn't believe that God loved her. How could she? She had yet to really truly see His love.

Have faith. Faith. Cassidy sighed and put her head in her hands. Faith in what? Her faith was shaky at best, nonexistent at worst.

"God, I can't see You, I can't feel You, and sometimes I feel like if You're there, You just take delight in making life difficult. I want to believe, but I don't think I can." She sighed and stood up. She turned off all the lights and made sure she had locked the doors. Her grandpa had always laughed at her need to lock up and told her that she had lived in the city for too long.

She got ready for bed, turned off the lights, and slipped under the covers. She lay there staring into the dark. "God, I'm not sure if I should do this or not, but I need to know You're real. If I'm going to make this commitment and raise Eric in the church, I need to believe in You, and I don't have the faith for that right now. If You're there, help me to not feel alone at church tomorrow. I'm tired of feeling like I'm fighting through life by myself." She turned her head towards her pillow as the tears slipped down her cheeks.

******

Cassidy had timed it so that she would get to the church just as it started. She didn't have many nice clothes so she had worn her nicest pair of jeans and a white sweater. She had curled the ends of her long hair and slipped into her newest pair of boots. Eric had grumbled all morning as they got ready, but he had found his nicest clothes as well. She had grabbed her grandpa's Bible and took a deep breath before heading out the door.

She got to the church and slipped in the door, hoping to go unnoticed, but there was a man there in a suit that gave her a warm smile, shook her hand and handed her a bulletin. She gave a weak smile back and hurried into the auditorium to slip into the back pew. Eric had seen a friend and raced off to join him. The music had started, and everyone was on their feet. She took a deep breath to try to calm her racing heart. The songs were unfamiliar to her so she stayed quiet, but she listened to the words. Before long, her heart quieted. The final song was starting when she felt someone slip into the pew next to her. She glanced over and found Jean Thompson giving her a warm smile. Next to her was Dylan. His look was not only welcoming, but compassionate as well. Cassidy smiled softly.

As the song ended, someone slipped in on her other side. She looked over and saw Gerri Hutchinson. Gerri leaned over and whispered, "I thought I'd never get here! That calf did not want to be born!" Cassidy stifled a laugh.

The worship leader encouraged the congregation to greet each other, and the family in front of her turned around. She saw the look of surprise cross their faces, but it quickly changed to genuine warmth.

"It's so nice to have you here." Warren Clifford had helped her numerous times on the ranch. It didn't surprise her that he was at church. He might be the only neighbor who had shown her true compassion. "We've been praying for you to join us."

"You have?" Cassidy was dumbfounded.

"Absolutely. Ray always asked us to pray for you, and we've never stopped." Warren's wife Karen grasped Cassidy warmly. "He loved you, and he wanted the best for you."

"Oh, well, thank you." Cassidy didn't know what to say or think. The warmth that they had shown her went beyond anything she had expected, and that they had prayed for her was an absolute shock. Maybe not everyone in town believed the rumors or had gossiped about her.

The Cliffords turned back around as the service began, and everyone took their seats. Cassidy didn't really pay attention to the sermon much. She was much too involved in her own thoughts. She had prayed that she wouldn't feel alone at church, and here she was surrounded by people who had shown her friendship and love. She struggled to keep her emotions in check, but she felt dangerously close to tears. She couldn't believe that God had answered her prayer. She certainly hadn't deserved it.

The service ended, and the Cliffords turned back to Cassidy. "It really was wonderful to see you here. I hope we see you back soon," Karen told her.

"And if you need any help with anything whatsoever, let me know," Warren added. "We're neighbors. You're not going through life alone."

Cassidy blinked back tears and thanked them. Hearing her own words come back at her made her realize that the reason she felt alone wasn't because she had no one around who cared, but because she had carefully kept them out of her life to avoid being hurt. Instead, she had hurt herself.

Gerri squeezed her hand. "I've got to go, but I'm so

glad you thought about what I said. I think you'll find that most people aren't as heartless as you think." Gerri grabbed her purse and slipped out of the pew.

Eric quickly took Dr. Hutchinson's place beside his mom. "Can I go over to Will's house?" He looked at her eagerly nearly dancing in his excitement.

"No, sir. You're still grounded, remember?" Eric flopped down on the pew and stuck out his lip. She was certain that he had no idea how childish he looked, or he never would have done it.

She felt a touch on her arm and turned towards the Thompsons. "We were wondering if you could join us for lunch," Jean said with a pleasant smile on her face. "I have some chili in the crockpot, some corn bread and I'll have a lettuce salad, too."

"I don't want to impose."

"Were we imposing when you let us stay with you for dinner the other night?" Cassidy felt a smile turn the corners of her mouth.

"Of course not. Okay, we'll come. Can I bring anything?"

"Everything is taken care of. Just bring Eric and yourself over." Jean gave Cassidy the directions.

"I'll go home and pick up Carlie," Dylan added. The immediate change to Eric's countenance was comical. He leaped out of the pew with a large smile on his face and nearly shoved his mom out of the way in his eagerness to get near the new owner of his beloved dog.

"Really? Can I play with her this afternoon?"

"If your mom says it's all right." Dylan looked at Cassidy, and she was happy that he had deferred to her. Eric also turned to face her, his heart in his eyes pleading with her.

"Of course. That would be fine." Cassidy knew that she

couldn't deny him the opportunity to play with the collie. She wondered if maybe it was time to think about giving him a dog of his own.

"We'll see you in a little bit," Dylan said with a smile before they too eased out of the pew.

Cassidy picked up her stuff and headed out of the pew as well. She was stopped before she reached the door by a couple of women. Instinctively, she pulled Eric close to her knowing that they weren't about to give her the warm welcome she had already experienced. One was older than the other, but both had bleached blonde hair with dark roots showing. The younger woman was wearing a dress that was a little too tight and pushed her cleavage out the top.

"It's so nice to see you in church," the younger woman said insincerely. She looked over at Eric with a sneer. "Sometimes I guess it takes a – an error of judgment – to make someone see the light, so to speak."

Cassidy pulled herself up a bit taller, but didn't seem to feel the need to reply. Eric's head dropped to his chest, and Cassidy had all she could do to push back the urge to protect her son by slapping the lady's nasty smile off her face.

"Church is the best place to put the fear of God into the young folks," the other lady jumped in. "Remind them that hell is real, and it's full of little sinners." She glared at Eric with enough venom that Cassidy pulled her son tighter. The way she was acting one would have thought that she had been the victim instead of Dylan.

"Well, now, we can't blame the children for the sins of their mothers – or fathers. Sometimes they just don't know any better." The woman smiled wickedly at Cassidy. "Wouldn't you agree, Miss Golden?" The stress on the miss was undeniable.

Before Cassidy could reply, the door to the church

opened, and Dylan walked back in. "I'm so sorry I took so long, Cassidy, but I'm ready whenever you are." He tipped his cowboy hat at the malicious women. "Ladies, I know you're enjoying getting to know our neighbor and showing her what Christian love looks like, but she has already agreed to have lunch with my mother and me. I'm sure you'll find another time to take her out and show her some Christian hospitality." He placed his hand on Cassidy's back and gently propelled her towards the door. The women's jaws had dropped, and although they had the grace to look embarrassed by their behavior, Cassidy was sure that they would eagerly dissect this new tidbit thrown at their feet.

They stepped into the brisk air, and Cassidy pulled away from Dylan to slip on her coat. "I can't thank you enough for coming in there. I don't know what I would have done if I had to listen to their vicious tongues a second longer." Cassidy seethed with anger. "How did you know I needed you?"

Dylan scuffed the toe of his boot on the ground. "Someone from church told me that they were heading your directions. Knowing those two like I do, I figured that they might not have the best intentions in mind." He glanced up at Cassidy. "Just remember two things. Not everyone that goes to church is a Christian, and even if they are, we're all still sinners. Don't expect perfection."

Cassidy nodded. "I suppose you're right. Thank you for the reminder." She headed to her SUV and climbed inside with Eric. Taking a deep breath she tried to purge the unpleasantness from her mind and remind herself of the ways God had answered her prayers. She looked in the rear view and saw Eric hunched over in his seat. "They don't know what they're saying, you know."

Eric shrugged. "I brought it on myself. I knew better,

but I did it anyway." He glanced up with his eyes on fire. "But they had no right to blame you for what I did. I didn't even think about how it would make people treat you." He eyes shimmered with tears for a moment. "I'm sorry, Mom."

Cassidy smiled. "I'm a big girl. I can take care of myself. Just remember next time you're tempted to do wrong that your decision effects more than just you, deal?"

Eric smiled. "Deal."

"All right. Let's go see Carlie." Cassidy put the car in gear and headed to Mrs. Thompson's house.

The Launch

Dylan followed Cassidy's SUV for a few blocks before turning to head to his home to pick up Carlie. He was thankful for the person who had alerted him to what was going on in the church foyer so that he could go help Cassidy. Penny and Hayley Carter had tendency to be malicious gossips. He wondered what they had said to Cassidy and Eric and then decided that it was better that he didn't know. He may just have turned back around and given them a piece of his mind. As it was, he hoped they choked on his insincere words. Unfortunately, he figured that they would just tear both of them apart after they had left.

Dylan took a deep breath and rolled his shoulders back trying to shed the tightness that had taken over them. He thought back to Cassidy asking how he had known that she needed him. He had needed to look away from her for a moment, because all of a sudden he had wanted her to need him. Not to be rescued from bitter women, but just to have him in her life. It had taken him by surprise. There was something vulnerable about Cassidy, and yet she gave him the feeling that she could take on anything life threw at her. And according to his mom, life had thrown some hard balls her way.

He pulled up in front of his house. Unlocking the door, he was met immediately by Carlie. The dog had become a favorite at the store in just a matter of days, but it was watching Eric work with her that made him feel like he had made the right decision. He ruffed up Carlie's fur in welcome then opened the door for her to head outside. "Wanna go to Mom's house, girl?" The dog barked in excitement and dashed out to the truck. She waited patiently until Dylan opened the door and then eagerly jumped inside. He climbed in the driver's seat and began to drive. He knew she would like the window down, but it was a bit too cold for him to allow that, even on a short drive.

Looking at Carlie reminded him of Eric. The boy had impressed him as he had worked the store. He had done everything Dylan had asked and done it well. If he wasn't sure of something he asked questions, which was a valuable skill to have. Carlie shadowed Eric everywhere around the store, and Dylan had been impressed that Eric still kept to his task even though he was sure the boy would rather play with the dog. It was a shame that Eric hadn't done things differently, because the dog and boy belonged together. He understood why Cassidy didn't feel like she could allow him to keep the dog though. If he were a parent, he probably would have done the same thing.

Then again, if Eric hadn't made the choice he had, Dylan wouldn't have met the family. He found it hard to believe that he had known them less than a week. He already felt such a strong tie to them. He felt like he would jump in and fight their battles if they needed him to. He felt like he could spend every day with them and still look forward to seeing them again tomorrow. He felt like – he felt like he wanted them to be part of his family. He began breathing fast as he reached that conclusion. It couldn't be possible, could it? He didn't love them – because marrying

Cassidy would require that he love them both – did he? He shook his head. Of course not! It wasn't possible. He hadn't known them long enough for this to be love. Still as he pulled up in his mom's driveway, he found himself anticipating time with the two of them. It might not be love yet, but he was aware that it could easily turn into love. He tried to push the thought out of his mind as he climbed out of the truck and let Carlie out. The dog bounded to the front door which was thrown open by Eric. The boy and dog greeted each other as if they hadn't seen each other in weeks instead of a couple days, and Dylan had to smile as he watched the two of them.

"Thank you for bringing Carlie over, Mr. Thompson," Eric said without looking up from the dog.

Dylan's smile broadened. "I think Carlie is just as happy to see you as you are to see her. Why don't we all go inside? I don't know about you, but I'm hungry."

Eric and Carlie dashed into the house. Dylan found Cassidy placing the final pieces of silverware on the dining room table. He could hear his mom in the kitchen. Lunch smelled amazing, and his stomach growled in anticipation.

Cassidy looked up with a laugh. "That was impressive!"

Dylan smiled sheepishly. "Nothing like Mom's cooking to bring out the beast in a man."

Cassidy laughed even harder. "I'll have to remember that. It may come in handy someday."

Dylan found himself staring at her. This was the most relaxed he had ever seen her. Always before there had been tension, worry, anger, sadness, loneliness, but never had he seen her happy. Cassidy caught him looking at her and grew uncomfortable. She smoothed her hand over her hair. "What? Do I have something on my face?" she asked.

Dylan nodded. "Yeah. You have a smile on your face. I'm not sure I've seen it there before."

Cassidy's lips twitched. "Yeah, well, it probably hasn't been there much lately. Hopefully, that will all change. I think I kind of missed it."

Jean came in with oven mitts on and placed a pan of corn bread in the center of the table. Cassidy brought in a bowl of salad. "Dylan, can you go get the bowls of chili and bring them in?" Jean asked.

"Is there anything else I can grab?" Cassidy asked, eager to help.

"Why don't you go grab Eric? By the time you pull him away from the dog, I'm sure we'll be ready." Jean followed her son into the kitchen and grabbed a pitcher of ice water.

"She seems happier today," Dylan commented as his picked up two bowls of steaming chili off the kitchen island.

"Yes, she does," Jean agreed with a smile. "She's becoming a new woman right in front of our eyes. A Christmas miracle."

Dylan hadn't thought much about Christmas this year. Without snow it seemed odd that it was coming upon them. He saw the decorations, and heard the music, but it hadn't really registered. "I guess it could be," he admitted.

"It will be." Jean sounded confident as she walked back into the dining room. Dylan followed her and set his burdens on the table while she filled the glasses on the table. He returned for the other two bowls and returned by the time Cassidy and Eric came in and took their places at the table.

The lunch was full of laughter and getting to know each other better. The more Dylan got to know Cassidy and Eric, the more he liked them. He had begun to look forward to Eric coming in to the feed store every day. He hadn't known what to expect, but he had been pleasantly surprised. Even Wayne and Zach had told him that they were pleased with Eric's work.

Dylan still didn't know Cassidy well, but every time he found out something new about her, he liked it. She kept her cards close to her chest, but he didn't blame her for it. Given her history and the way Snowfall had welcomed her, it was understandable that trust didn't come easy for her.

Cassidy started to help clean up after dinner, but Jean wouldn't hear of it. She told Cassidy to go into the living room, and asked Eric to help to clean up. To his credit, Eric quickly stood up and pitched in. Even though Dylan knew Eric had looked forward to playing with Carlie, he didn't complain at all. Dylan started to help, but his mom stopped him.

"You can go keep Cassidy company. I have all the help I need," she said, patting Eric's arm.

Dylan glanced at his mom suspiciously. Was she trying to make a match between the two of them? Jean's face was the picture of innocence, and Dylan thought that maybe he was overreacting. She probably just didn't want Cassidy sitting in a room by herself. Jean had always had a soft spot for boys. She always made them feel like they belonged at her house.

Dylan followed Cassidy into the living room. She immediately was drawn to the mantle where a nativity set held the place of honor. She picked up the wooden Mary and studied it. "This is beautiful," she said, her finger tracing the lines of the girl's face.

"My dad carved that set." Dylan had always loved that set himself, probably because of all the memories he had of it.

Cassidy looked at him in surprise. "Your dad did this? It's amazing."

Dylan beamed. "The story goes that my mom had an expensive porcelain set that I loved to play with as a toddler, but of course, she wouldn't let me. So dad said that he would make her a set that I could play with without them being worried about it. The next Christmas, he gave her that set."

Cassidy was studying the pieces. "I wouldn't let a toddler play with this set either. It's too intricate and there was too much time invested."

Dylan went and stood next to her at the mantle. He picked up a shepherd and looked at it lovingly. "Apparently my mom agreed with you, because I wasn't allowed to play with this set either." He chuckled. "Dad was mad. He said that he had made it so that I could play with it, but Mom insisted that it was too nice to allow a toddler to drool on, throw, and break."

"So what did they do?" Cassidy placed the figure carefully back in the stable.

"Mom let me play with the porcelain set. I broke several figurines and she never complained. That set didn't have as much value to her anymore."

Cassidy looked around the room and finally spotted the porcelain set on an end table. Joseph had been obviously glued back together, the angel was missing a wing, and there was only one wise man. She laughed as she picked up the angel. "I'd say you had a good time with this set."

"Yeah, I did, but I always liked the set my dad made better."

"So do you carve?" Cassidy asked as she replaced the angel.

"No, I never picked up that skill. Dad tried to teach me, but I could never get the hang of it." Dylan held up his hand and pointed to a faint scar. "Got that when I was trying to learn though. My dad told me not to worry because chicks dig scars." He shook his head sadly. "I've never had one girl swoon over that scar though."

Cassidy laughed. "Poor thing."

Eric and Jean came in with Carlie faithfully following behind. "Can I go outside with Carlie, Mom?" Eric came over and leaned against his mother.

She smiled as she brushed his hair off his forehead lovingly. "It's all right with me as long as it's okay with Mrs. Thompson."

Eric looked over at Jean with his eyes wide and pleading. Jean laughed. "I've seen that look a million times kiddo. Go ahead. Enjoy it while you can. They're finally predicting snow in our forecast."

Eric shouted with joy and began to race towards the front door. "Don't forget your jacket!" Cassidy hollered after him.

"I'll come with you," Dylan stated, following the boy outside.

******

Cassidy smiled over at Jean. "We've been admiring your Christmas decorations. I haven't even got mine up yet. Somehow it doesn't feel like Christmas should be so close."

"I know it! One of my favorite movies is White Christmas and somehow it just doesn't seem right for there not to be any snow during Christmas." Jean thought for a moment. "Although I suppose I'd better get used to it, because I'm going to visit my sister in Arizona for Christmas this year, and I'm guessing there won't be any snow."

Cassidy chuckled. "It'd be funny if you got snow while you were there while we had to do without."

Jean smiled weakly. She crossed to the sofa and sat down. "I'm still not sure I should be going," she admitted. "I hate leaving Dylan all alone during the holidays. We have no family nearby, and he's been so busy with the store that he doesn't have any close friends who would take him in."

Cassidy was silent for a moment. She certainly wouldn't mind having Dylan join them for Christmas, but their holiday was small and quiet. She wasn't sure if he would enjoy it.

Jean misinterpreted her silence. "I hope you don't think I was trying to convince you to take Dylan in for Christmas. I was just talking out loud. It's a bad habit." She smiled.

"No, it's not that. I was thinking that he would be more than welcome to come to our place, but we have a very small Christmas. I don't know if it would be something he would want to do." Cassidy smiled. "If he brought Carlie with him, Eric would be ecstatic."

Jean smiled. "Well, it's only been Dylan and me for Christmas for many years so I don't think he'd be looking for anything elaborate."

"True. You guys have been in a similar situation as us – just a mom and her son for the holidays." Cassidy looked at the ground for a moment. Gathering her resolve she moved over to the sofa and sat down. "Do you ever find it difficult to celebrate with it being just the two of you? Like the effort isn't worth it?"

Jean nodded slowly. "Especially when my husband first died. But there's one difference in our situations. Dylan was the one who carried on with the holiday traditions to try to cheer me up for several years, while I think you probably feel like you have to carry on for Eric. It's only been recently that I've sort of gotten back into the swing of – life, I guess."

Cassidy awkwardly placed her hand on Jean's arm and patted it to try to show some sympathy. "It's hard. I didn't realize how hard it would be."

"Harder than the situation you were in?" Jean studied her face.

"No. That was also a hard time. But leaving was difficult. I knew that there was a chance that he would follow us, and if he found us I didn't know what he would do." Cassidy looked up at Jean with tears shimmering in her eyes. "I felt so guilty when I heard he had died, because I had prayed that God would do anything to keep him from finding us. When I heard Brad had been killed, I felt so relieved and even happy. I felt like a terrible person."

"I think you were a very normal person. It would be hypocritical to act like you were sad about the death of someone who had hurt you and Eric repeatedly. Relief to be forever free of his abuse and fear would have driven out any trace of sadness."

Cassidy wiped her hands together nervously. "I felt responsible for his death."

"How could it possibly have been your fault?"

With eyes brimming with tears, Cassidy said, "Because I know he was looking for us. He had been out drinking when we left. When he came home and found us gone, he took off after us. That's when he got in his accident."

Jean rubbed her shoulder. "Oh, honey, you can't take responsibility for that. It was his choice to drive when he was impaired. He drove home in the same condition. That was his decision, not yours."

Cassidy nodded, and then decided that it was time to change the subject. She shifted on the couch and faced Jean. "So, I'll go ahead and invite Dylan to Christmas, and if he accepts you won't have to worry about him while you're visiting your sister."

"That sounds like an excellent plan." Jean smiled warmly, and Cassidy was reminded of her own mother in that moment. Before Cassidy could react, Jean continued. "It was so nice to see you in church today. I hope that you'll continue to join us."

Cassidy smiled. "It's funny. I had been so nervous last night that I would be shunned or just alone that I prayed to the Lord that I wouldn't be by myself. Then He sent you and Dylan to me, and Dr. Hutchinson and the Cliffords, and you were all so welcoming and friendly. It was lovely." Her face clouded over for a moment. "Most of it was lovely."

"What happened?" Jean spoke with such concern that Cassidy soon found herself pouring out the story of the two women who had made their antagonism so abundantly clear. Jean compressed her lips. "I know exactly who you are talking about. That would be Penny and Hayley Carter. They're mother and daughter, and you know the saying about the apple not falling far from the tree. Penny has some – interesting ideas of what Christianity looks like. She reminds me of the Pharisees in a lot of ways. Quick to judge others, but can't see her own shortcomings." Jean sighed. "Unfortunately, she also can't see the failings of her precious daughter. Hayley would never measure up to her mother's standards, but Penny overlooks them." Jean eyed Cassidy carefully for a moment. "Hayley probably has a more particular interest in you though. She's been after Dylan for years, but he has never even noticed it. You're competition."

Cassidy's eyes widened, and she jumped off the couch. "Oh no, I'm not! We barely know each other. We're friends – more like acquaintances - but that's all."

Jean stood as well, but she had a smile on her face. "I know that, and Dylan knows that, but to Hayley you're a single woman who has suddenly become very involved in Dylan's life." Jean laughed. "I would have given anything to have seen her face when Dylan came to your rescue!"

Cassidy placed her hands over her face in embarrassment. She groaned. "I was hoping to put to rest all the rumors that were circling about me. Instead I've probably created more."

Jean put her arm around Cassidy's shoulders. "In this town we've all had rumors spread about us. After my husband died, people were saying that I worked him to death, and that my depression was caused by the guilt I felt knowing that I could have prevented his death. And while it was true that I struggled with depression following his death, it wasn't guilt. My husband had a blockage that caused his heart attack. I don't think there's a single person in town that hasn't had some sort of gossip about them."

Cassidy lifted her head. "What about Dylan?"

Jean removed her arm and took a step back. She sighed heavily. "With him being single and not seeming to be interested in any of the women around here, he's had plenty of gossip about him, too." She left it vague allowing Cassidy's imagination to fill in all the rumors that could fly around a situation like that. "I'm telling you, we've all been there, and if we haven't, it'll happen soon enough."

Cassidy walked over to the mantle and picked up the wooden carving of Jesus. She lovingly stroked his little face. "The worst one was when Eric came home crying, because the kids had told him that I wasn't really Ray's granddaughter. Instead I was his mistress, a gold digger claiming that Eric was his child. They said that Ray had taken me and Eric in out of guilt, but made up the story of me being his granddaughter to protect his reputation. Eric was crushed."

Jean smiled sadly. "I heard that one, too, but no one who truly knew your grandfather believed it. Ray was too wise to be taken in by a young gold digger, and he loved your grandma too much to have a mistress." Jean folded her arms across her stomach. "I'm sorry that things have been so rough since you moved here. I'm surprised you haven't packed your bags and left."

Cassidy placed the wooden figure back on the mantle and laughed shortly. "Where would I go? I had no money, no family, and Grandpa had made me promise not to sell the ranch for at least ten years after his death. He didn't want me to make a hasty decision that I would regret later."

Jean nodded. "That sounds like Ray. He loved that ranch. He would have wanted it to remain in the family if at all possible."

Cassidy put her hands in her pockets. "He did. I think that's why he was so hurt when my dad said that he didn't want the ranch."

"Is that what their big fight was about?" Jean leaned forward intently. Cassidy could tell that Jean had wanted to know this information for a while.

"It really wasn't a big fight. I know the town thinks that there was some huge grudge between my father and grandpa, but it wasn't like that." Cassidy smiled at her memories. "Dad told Grandpa that he wanted to be an actor. Grandpa thought it was a stupid idea especially since the ranch was so profitable and obviously where the family belonged. But Dad left anyway. He spent most of his life like most actors – waiting tables." Cassidy chuckled. "But he was happy. Mom worked in a retail store, and so between the two of them we had enough for our needs, but not a lot of extras. So Grandpa would come visit us since we couldn't afford the trip to see him. He told me lots of stories about the ranch, and I couldn't wait to see it." She sighed. "Now I couldn't leave even if I wanted to."

Jean sat down on the edge of the couch. "Do you?"

Cassidy looked at her in confusion. "Do I what?"

"Want to leave?"

Cassidy looked at the ground for a moment, gathering her thoughts. Did she want to leave? Sometimes, yes she very much wanted to leave the care, the worry, the town behind. "Sometimes it crosses my mind, but at the end of the day I love the ranch almost as much as my grandpa did. I know I'd miss it."

The door opened, and they could hear Eric and Dylan wiping their feet and the jingle of Carlie's tags. They soon appeared in the living room with pink cheeks and sparkling eyes. Eric flopped down on the couch and Carlie plopped down on the floor beside him with a contented sigh. "Got anything warm for a couple of frozen boys, Mom?" Dylan asked.

Jean popped up off the couch. "Of course I do. I should have thought of it before." As she left, Cassidy started to follow her. "I can do it by myself. You stay here." She nodded over to where Dylan was crouched to pet Carlie. Cassidy knew that Jean wouldn't let her get out of asking Dylan to Christmas, but with her new found information about some of the women in this town, she was second guessing her offer. She didn't know if she hoped he would say yes or no. She wiped her hands on her jeans and took a step toward Dylan.

"Your mom said that she's going to be in Arizona for Christmas this year," she started.

Dylan looked up with a smile. "Yeah, it's going to be good for her to get away for a bit. It's been awhile since she's seen her sister."

Cassidy took a deep breath. "If you don't have other plans you could join us for Christmas."

Dylan stood up slowly. He watched Cassidy's face intently for a few moments. "Did my mom ask you to invite me over? I told her I'd be fine."

"No, no of course not. I just thought that since you'd

101

be alone, and we only have the two of us, that maybe you could join us. It's not going to be anything big." As Dylan continued to hesitate, Cassidy grew more nervous. Her words started tumbling out on top of each other. "You don't have to come. I mean we'll be fine. We're always fine. And I know you'll be fine, too. I know you probably have other friends you'd rather be with. I mean, we're practically strangers."

Dylan put up his hand to halt her voice. He smiled warmly. Wow, he had a nice smile. Had she noticed that before? "I'd love to spend Christmas with you and Eric. I just didn't want my mom to pressure you into asking me." He looked down at Carlie. "I'm assuming it would be all right if I bring her as well."

Eric surged to his feet. "Of course. Carlie is always welcome! It'll be the best Christmas ever!"

Dylan smiled at Eric and mussed his hair. "Oh, now that I'm bringing the dog you're excited, but when it was just me there was no excitement over that. I see how it is."

Eric blushed. "No, it's not that, it's just . . ."

"It's all right, Eric. I know Carlie's a lot of fun." Eric looked relieved that he didn't have to explain himself and dropped to the floor by the dog to avoid any more questions. Dylan looked up at Cassidy. "So it's all set. Carlie and I will be happy to spend Christmas with you."

Cassidy felt her heart race and wondered if she had made a wise decision.

The Prayer

When Cassidy got home and had put Eric to bed, she went back into the living room. She was glad that her grandpa had taught her how to lay the fire, because it warmed the room nicely. Plus there was something comforting about the crackle of a fire. Normally she would turn on the television and find something to fill the time before climbing into bed. Sometimes she would read, but tonight nothing was holding her interest.

She sat and stared into the fire thinking about the events of the day. God had answered her prayer. She couldn't deny it. She had been pleased to see Eric find a friend right off, and with the Clifford family there, that meant that his friend, Wyatt, would be there as well. She had carefully asked him about church when she had put him to bed. Eric was her primary concern, and if he wasn't being treated well, she wanted to know right away. Eric's response had brought a smile to her face though.

"Oh, Mom! You worry too much. Other than that one crazy rumor I heard a few years ago, I didn't even know there were rumors about us. The kids have always been nice to me, and it turns out that most of my close friends from school also go to church." He smiled. "It was kind of cool hanging out with them, especially since I'm grounded."

"Feel like you got away with something, huh?" Cassidy couldn't help, but smile back. "I'm glad that you enjoyed your time at church. I really feel like it would be good for us to be more involved in the community. Get to know some more people. We're kind of isolated out here."

"No, Mom. You're isolated out here. I have friends, because I go to school. You only have me." Cassidy was shocked by her son's insight, but even more stunned by the truth of it. Eric did have friends. In spite of the rumors, he was constantly being invited to parties, to friends' homes, to go hang out. Why hadn't she noticed this?

In the dim room, she asked herself the question once more. Why hadn't she noticed that Eric had friends in the community, but she didn't? The gossip and stories didn't seem to bother Eric, but they made her hide herself away. Maybe the town wasn't filled with malicious people that were out to get her. Maybe they were just normal people in a normal town. Gossip was going to be present, but it didn't mean that everyone believed it. Her actions may have inadvertently given the stories more fuel. If she had been willing to be part of the town, maybe they would have gotten to know her and found out the truth. By hiding, she may seem to be verifying the lies.

"Oh Lord, have I hurt myself trying to protect myself?"

I will protect you. Cassidy stopped breathing. The voice hadn't been audible, yet she was certain that God was answering her.

"I guess I should have trusted You."

Trust in the Lord with all your heart, and lean not on your own understanding.

"Yeah, I know. I'm sorry, Lord." Her eyes burned with unshed tears. "I've certainly made a mess of things. I want to lean on You and have You direct my paths. You'll certainly do a better job than me." She paused. "Thank You for providing support for me on my first day back to church. It was nice to have some friendly faces around me." She frowned and sighed. "Please don't allow my encounter with the Carter women to hurt Dylan in any way. Help them to see the truth."

Somehow she knew that God had heard her, even though she didn't hear an answer. She also knew that the answer may not look the way she wanted it to look. She pushed up from her seat and banked the fire before heading to bed. She felt more at rest than she had in a long time and knew she would sleep well knowing that God was in control.

The Gossip

Dylan hadn't been at the feed store long the next day when Hayley Carter arrived. He could tell she was on a mission the minute she stepped foot in the store. He tried to sneak into his office before she spotted him, but she had zeroed in on him like a hawk swooping in for its prey. He forced a smile on his face and decided to get it over with.

"Good morning, Miss Carter. What can I help you with?"

"Oh, I'm here to help you," she said with a smile that made his skin crawl. She positioned herself to best show off her figure, and Dylan bit his cheeks as the image of her practicing this position in the mirror came to mind. He briefly wondered what other positions had been rehearsed and thrown out in favor of this one. She looked unnatural, and while he was sure that there were men who would be unable to resist looking at her, it only made him more determined to keep his eyes on her face. He wouldn't give her the satisfaction.

"You are? That's interesting. What do you think you could help me with?" Dylan had a feeling he knew exactly what she was there for. After he had called her and her mother out yesterday at church he had expected that one or both of them would come chew him out.

She leaned closer to him, and he took a step back,

but found himself backed up against a shelf. How had he managed to get himself cornered? "Why don't we go into your office where it's more private?"

Dylan shook his head immediately. He knew Hayley didn't always stick to the truth, and he wanted there to be witnesses to anything that might be said or done between them. "Anything you have to say to me can be said right here."

Hayley looked shocked, but then she shrugged. "If you don't mind, I don't either. I think you ought to know that there are rumors going around that you and that Golden woman are an item. I know it isn't true, but when you sit beside her in church and then take her to lunch, people will start talking." She placed her hand on his arm. He glanced down and frowned at her long red nails and gaudy cheap rings. "You may want to be more careful about how things look."

He slid sideways getting her to remove her hand from his arm. The move also improved his position so he could angle himself away from the shelf. He now had a way to leave if necessary. "Well, thanks for letting me know. I think that most people will understand that my family has been friends with the Golden family for a long time, and that we wanted them to feel welcomed at church. And if they did pair me up with her, I don't think that would be the worst person they could put me with." He stared at her and wondered how someone got to be so mean spirited. "Besides, I wasn't sitting next to her in church, my mom was, and she went to my mom's house for lunch. The story has already got its facts twisted. I know that you'll correct anyone who has it wrong."

She tossed her hair over her shoulder. "Well, if you're not going to take it seriously, then I guess I've wasted my time."

Dylan laughed. "If I took every rumor seriously, I'd be in trouble."

"There is a way to put that particular rumor to bed quickly." She lowered her eyelashes and then looked up at him, and again Dylan had the idea that she had practiced the look in the mirror. He felt his lips twitch, but his amusement quickly faded when she placed a hand on his chest. He backed up quickly. "You could take me out, and then everyone will know that you couldn't possibly be interested in her."

Dylan grabbed her hand and pushed it away from him. "It's nice of you to sacrifice yourself like that, but again, I'm not worried about the rumor." He hoped that his disgust wasn't apparent.

Hayley pouted. "You can't tell me you would prefer her over me."

Dylan sighed. "I didn't say that. All I said was that I wasn't concerned about the rumors. If the town wants to talk about my love life, then they're hitting the bottom of the barrel because it's literally nonexistent."

"It wouldn't have to be," she purred.

"I want it to be." He was growing tired of the conversation, and not feeling pleasant any longer. He placed his hands on her shoulders. "I appreciate your concern, but I'm a grown up and I think I can handle my life without any interference. I've tried to be nice about it, but apparently you need me to be blunt. I'm not interested in you. I don't want to go out with you. Honestly, given the choice between the two of you, I'd pick Cassidy." He watched as her face paled at his words. He felt like a jerk, but he was so tired of her not getting his not-so-subtle hints.

She drew herself up proudly. "Fine. I was only trying to help you." She turned on her heel and marched towards the door. Her dignified exit was ruined when she caught her heel on the rug and stumbled, but she recovered quickly and ran out.

Dylan laughed as soon as she was out of earshot, but not for long. Zach headed his direction. "I think you just made an enemy," he said worriedly. "She's been after you for a long time."

"I know. She wouldn't take a hint so I decided to speak plainly." Dylan chewed his lip. "Maybe I should have been gentler."

Zach shrugged. "Don't think it would have matter. Hayley does not like it when she doesn't get her way. She'll make you pay or she'll make that girl pay – the one she thinks you like."

Dylan shifted. "Unfortunately, you're probably right." A customer went up to the counter, and Zach left to go help him. Dylan decided that he needed some privacy to think things over. He went into his office and shut the door. Sitting in his creaky old chair, he put his feet up on his desk and tilted back.

He knew that many people thought he was unaware of Hayley's interest in him, but she had been more than obvious. He knew what she wanted, but he wasn't willing to give it to her. He hadn't wanted to hurt her though, so he had tried to discourage her gently. She just wouldn't take a hint though. He had hated having to spell it out for her, but he was tired of trying to duck out of her sight and cringing every time he saw her coming.

Well, he had fixed that. She definitely wouldn't be interested in him anymore. But Zach was right. She wouldn't let it go that easily, especially since there had been more than one person who could have heard the whole thing. Her tongue was vicious, and he knew that she could spread things around town quickly. He wasn't too concerned about himself. He had a good reputation, and most people would immediately dismiss anything against him as false. It was Cassidy that concerned him. There were enough that believed the rumors about her already that one more wasn't going to be too hard to believe. He hated that just when she was opening up and venturing out of the fortress she had created for herself at the ranch that something like this would happen.

He frowned. His boring life had certainly gotten interesting since Eric had stepped foot in the store. Although he knew he should be frustrated by the upheaval that family had brought to his life, instead he felt happiness and excitement. He looked forward to his time with them, and when that time was done, he looked forward to the next time they would meet.

Dylan put his feet back on the ground. He needed to tell Cassidy what had happened. He decided that the conversation could take place face to face when he took Eric home that night. Yes, that was the perfect way to handle it. He smiled as he made the decision and got to work.

The Conversation

Cassidy balanced herself on the ladder before hammering the nail into the board. After seeing Jean's house decorated for Christmas, Cassidy had decided it was past time that she got her own decorations up. She had never hung lights on the outside of the house before, but Eric had begged her to every year. She made up her mind that this year she would finally do it. Perched on the ladder, though, she questioned her sanity. Heights had always frightened her, something that had only increased since her parent's plane crash.

The crunch of gravel alerted her that someone was coming. She wasn't surprised to recognize Dylan's truck coming down the driveway. He had texted her that he would bring Eric home. What did surprise her was the way her heart seemed to pick up speed knowing that she would be seeing him again. Even with Brad she hadn't felt this way.

She took a deep breath and carefully descended from the ladder, clutching the hammer tightly in one hand. She had barely reached solid ground when the truck stopped, and Eric flew out the passenger side.

"You're hanging Christmas lights?" he shouted excitedly. "Yes! Finally we get to have the house decorated! It's bad enough there hasn't been any snow, but without the

111

Christmas decorations, it's just been sad."

Cassidy looked at Eric in surprise. "You never said anything about wanting to get the Christmas things out."

Eric shrugged. "I didn't want to stress you out."

Cassidy looked in amazement from Eric to Dylan. Dylan laughed at her expression and reached for the hammer. "Here, let me help." He paused with his hand outstretched. "Unless you'd rather do it yourself."

Cassidy gladly thrust the hammer into his hand. "No, I'm terrified of heights. I will gladly let you take care of this. In the meantime, I'll get dinner finished up. You'll join us won't you?" She found herself holding her breath as she waited for his answer.

"Absolutely. It's the best offer I have tonight." He smiled and winked at her, and Cassidy took a deep breath.

"Great." She cleared her throat when the word came out sounding squeaky. "Eric, why don't you come inside as well?"

"Aw, Mom. Can't I help Mr. Thompson?" Eric whined.

"Do you still have homework to do?" Cassidy looked at her son pointedly. If the feed store wasn't busy, Dylan would allow Eric to work on his homework at the shop, but more often than not, Eric had work to finish when he got home.

Eric hung his head. "Fine," he muttered as he slowly mounted the porch steps.

Dylan chuckled. "We'll have to give him a manly chore to do after dinner to make up for that insult."

Cassidy looked at him quickly. The way he had said 'we' had sounded like a family, like he was part of them. "Yeah. I'm sure that would help ease the pain."

"You just want these lights around the edge of the house or were you thinking of something more fancy?"

"Well, since I wanted to spend the least amount of time

as possible on the ladder, I was thinking that I would trim the porch and then wrap some lights around the posts."

Dylan looked at the house and nodded. "Sounds like a good start. Next year, I can climb up on the roof and trim the whole house." He started up the ladder, a hammer and box of nails in one hand and a string of lights in the other.

Cassidy found her stomach clenching in fear just watching him. "I'm going inside now unless you need any help."

"I should be fine. I'll let you know if I need anything." He got to work, and Cassidy was relieved to step inside. She shook her head and got to work making hamburger patties and cooking French fries.

He had said 'we', and then he had mentioned 'next year'. She wondered if he had even noticed it. He was taking for granted that he would still be part of their lives next Christmas. Not only that, but taking on the task of decorating the house as if it were the most natural thing in the world. She was amazed at how quickly he had become a good friend – almost like family.

She imagined next Christmas, sitting in her living room with the fire going. Carlie would be asleep on the rug, basking in the warmth of the fire. In her thoughts, Eric would be excitedly looking through the presents under the tree, while Jean brought in a plate of cookies. Dylan would sit beside her and put his arm around her shoulder lovingly, and . . .

The smell of smoke brought her out of her day dream. She reached in the oven and quickly yanked out the tray of French fries. She breathed a sigh of relief when she saw that only a few of the smaller ones had burned, but the rest seemed fine. She opened some windows to let out the smoke and criticized herself for letting her mind wander. She got everything on the table and then called up the stairs

113

for Eric. She heard him barreling down the stairs as she stuck her head out to call Dylan in, but nearly ran smack into his chest. He caught her arms to keep her from running into him.

"Whoa. That was close. I guess we have pretty good timing." He smiled, and her heart fluttered. "I was just coming to tell you that I was done and have you look at the lights. I want to make sure it's what you wanted." He led Cassidy down the porch steps and turned her to face the house. He flipped a switch, and Cassidy felt her lips curve into a smile.

"It's perfect," she whispered.

Eric stood next to her. "It needs more lights," he said critically.

Dylan laughed as he put a hand on Eric's shoulders. "Sorry, buddy. That's all the lights we have. After Christmas we'll go to the store and buy out what they have left when they're on sale. Next year, this house will be jaw dropping."

"Yes!" Eric jumped in the air and gave Dylan a high five before running back inside.

Cassidy looked at Dylan. There it was again – 'we' and 'next year'. It seemed like Dylan had firmly planted himself into their family. She wasn't even sure that he had realized it yet, though. She took a deep breath. She wasn't sure she liked how quickly her heart raced when she thought about a future with Dylan. Why was she even thinking about a future with Dylan?

She shook her head to clear it from these bothersome thoughts. "Dinner is ready. Eric, go wash up."

Eric took off, and Cassidy followed along more slowly with Dylan. He had already taken down the ladder and placed it next to the porch with the hammer and nails. "I didn't know if you wanted to keep the boxes for the lights or not," he said. "My mom always liked to keep them, but my dad always thought they were a nuisance so he'd throw them away when Mom wasn't looking." Dylan chuckled at the memory.

Cassidy joined him. "I'm actually with your dad on this one. I can never seem to get them to fit back inside the box."

"I'll throw those away then. Where do the tools go? I can put them all away." They had reached the porch, and Dylan began picking up the empty boxes to put in the garbage.

Cassidy grabbed the hammer and nails. "I'll take these. I keep them inside, but if you could take the ladder out to the shed, that would be fantastic."

Dylan placed the trash in the can. "Got it." He shouldered the ladder.

"Do you need a flashlight?" Cassidy glanced out towards the darkened shed with some concern. The porch light didn't stretch that far and there was no electricity in the shed. Without waiting for a response, she replied. "Hold on a second." She didn't wait to see if he would listen to her before heading into the house. "Eric, I'm going with Dylan to the shed. Set the table." She placed the hammer and nails on the kitchen counter and reached into a drawer to grab a flashlight. She flicked it on to make sure it worked before heading back outside. She was relieved to see Dylan still standing where she had left him. He grinned at her and her heart did a flip.

"I tried to go by myself, but it's awfully dark out there. I figured it wouldn't do you any good if I turned my ankle in a hole or something." Dylan's eyes twinkled as he spoke.

"That wouldn't be good at all," she responded, flipping on the light and guiding his way to the shed. "I'm not sure Eric and I could get you to the house. We'd have to call an ambulance."

"That would certainly create a stir in town," Dylan agreed. "I'm sure they'd have a heyday with that one."

Cassidy snorted. "I'm sure they would say that I attacked you or something."

"Probably." They reached the shed, and Cassidy opened the doors. She shone the light on the place where the ladder was supposed to go and watched as Dylan replaced it with care. He turned back around, and Cassidy was surprised at how close he was in the small space. Startled, she took a step back and stepped wrong on the cement slab that the shed was built on. She yelped as she felt her ankle turn and fell onto her backside. Dylan rushed over to her, and she tried not to moan in embarrassment, but soon she was moaning for an entirely different reason. Her ankle throbbed in pain.

"Are you all right? What happened?" He clasped her hand and tried to help her up, but it was quickly apparent to Cassidy that she was not going to be able to walk on it.

She let out a small cry and leaned against him. "I didn't see the small step at the door and turned my ankle. It hurts." She wanted to be strong, to act like it wasn't worth mentioning, but she felt like she was going to throw up, and from the way her boot felt she was fairly certain that it was already starting to swell.

Dylan gently lowered her back to the ground and took the flashlight. He went down by her feet and felt her ankle, causing her to flinch in pain. "Sorry. I didn't mean to hurt you worse." He stood up. "I don't want to take your boot off, but I'm fairly certain you've got a sprain." He knelt down next to her. "Put your arms around my neck."

Cassidy looked at him in horror. "You're not going to carry me back to the house, are you?"

"Just do it! You can't walk back, and I can't leave you

116

here all night in December. So unless you want me to call that ambulance for you, put your arms around my neck." His frustration at her hesitation was clear. She hesitantly obeyed, hating that it had happened, that it had come to this. She was so embarrassed. He picked her up and carried her back to the house. By the time they got there, Cassidy was biting her lip to keep from smiling. This wasn't like the movies. Dylan was sweating in the cold and breathing hard after the exertion of carrying her. She could have sworn that he stifled a groan as he gently set her on the porch. He saw her grin and smiled sheepishly back at her. "Maybe the ambulance would have been better," he teased. Cassidy laughed, and Dylan chuckled along with her. "They make it look so easy in the movies."

"Well, I think most actresses weigh less than I do, and they only have to carry them a few seconds before the director will yell cut. It's all movie magic."

The door burst open, and Eric stepped out into the cold. "Are we going to eat or what? I'm starving!"

Dylan mussed Eric's hair. "Just a minute, buddy. Your mom hurt her ankle while we were putting the ladder away."

"Go ahead and dish up your plate," Cassidy suggested as she hopped over to the nearest chair at the kitchen table.

Eric watched his mom in concern. "Are you going to be okay?"

"Yeah, I think it's just a sprain. I'll be okay."

That was enough for Eric to relieve his mind, so he took his mom's advice and started dishing up his dinner. Dylan tried to gently remove Cassidy's boot, but he could tell that she was struggling to hide how much it hurt. He laid his hand on top of the one she had gripping the table. "It's okay to tell me that it hurts. I won't think less of you because you experience pain."

Cassidy looked at him for a moment. "It's not you," she said with a meaningful glance at Eric. She didn't want to worry her son so she had been trying to hide the pain for his sake. She saw comprehension dawn on Dylan's face.

"How attached are you to these boots?" he asked.

Cassidy groaned. "You're going to have to cut it off aren't you?" The conflict was apparent on her face, but finally resignation settled in. "Do what you have to do." These weren't her nice boots, but these were her every day boots. The ones that she didn't mind getting dirty and could wear all day long because they were comfortably broken in. Dylan stood up and was rummaging around in some cupboards for a while before he found some heavy duty shears. He cut through the leather as carefully as he could. Eric sat and watched wide-eyed, his food forgotten.

As he freed her foot, Dylan asked Eric to get a pillow. "Do you have any ibuprofen?" he asked Cassidy.

She nodded and told him where to find some in the medicine cabinet. Soon both of them were back. She lifted her foot gently to the pillow that Eric had placed on the chair next to her and dutifully took the medicine that Dylan gave her. Then he got a bag of ice, wrapped it in a towel and placed it gently on her swollen ankle.

With a sigh, Eric said, "Now can we eat?" Dylan and Cassidy laughed, but agreed that it was finally time to eat. Dylan kept Eric entertained through dinner, and Cassidy found herself enjoying how easily he spoke with her son. He didn't try to force friendship on him or lecture him. He was just incredibly nice to Eric and showed that he genuinely cared about him. It was something that Cassidy had wondered if she'd ever find in a man – someone who genuinely liked Eric. In that moment, Cassidy realized that she had been right to fear that she might fall for Dylan, but she had not been diligent enough because she had already fallen for him.

******

Dylan kept one eye on Cassidy throughout dinner. She was pale and every once in a while she would wince as she moved her foot. He was sure she was right, that it was just a sprain, but he knew she was still in pain and that the next few days were going to be difficult. He wanted to be around to help her, but knew that was impossible.

"Do you have crutches?" he asked suddenly. He could tell that she was caught off guard, but she recovered quickly.

"Actually, I think we have some from when my grandpa hurt his knee in a car accident. I think they're in the hall closet." Dylan got up from his chair and went to search the closet. He would feel a lot better leaving her alone if he knew she wasn't completely helpless. He found the crutches and was relieved to find that they were adjustable.

When he came back into the kitchen, Eric was clearing the table. The serious look on his face showed Dylan that he understood the situation, probably more than Cassidy would like him to. He was happy to see Eric helping out and hoped it would continue through the next few days.

He came over to Cassidy and removed the bag of ice. He helped her stand on her good foot and then handed her the crutches. He watched as she struggled with them for a moment. Taking them back, he readjusted them until they were perfect for her height.

"Let's go into the living room," Dylan suggested. Eric had finished cleaning up and he followed them, keeping a careful eye on his mom's progress. Dylan helped Cassidy into the recliner and lifted the foot rest so she could keep her feet up. "Is your bedroom upstairs?"

Cassidy's eyes widened. "Yes," she moaned. "There's

no way I'll be able to manage the stairs tonight."

"Don't worry, Mom. I know what to do." Eric took off up the stairs and soon came down with sheets, a pillow and blankets. He started to set up a bed on the couch. "It'll be nice. You can have the fire going, and you'll be nice and comfy."

Cassidy smiled warmly as she watched her son help her. Dylan looked away, feeling like he had seen something that wasn't intended for him. The moment had shaken him though, because he knew that he wanted to be part of this little family. He wanted to have the right to care for Cassidy and help train Eric. He wanted to celebrate holidays with them, mourn with them, work beside them. He caught his breath. Looking around the room frantically for something – anything – to change the train of his thoughts, his eyes landed on a box with an artificial Christmas tree.

"Were you going to set up your tree tonight?"

Cassidy groaned. "Well, that was the plan, but now it won't happen."

"Sure it will," Dylan said cheerfully. "Decorating may have to wait, but I can get it set up."

"I'll help," Eric eagerly volunteered. Together they got the tree put together and the lights hung on the boughs. Cassidy gave directions from her chair as she watched the two of them work side by side. Dylan wondered if she was thinking about what a nice family they made like he was, or if he was the only one enjoying the moment.

"Now for the decorations," Eric shouted as he pulled out a box from under the coffee table.

"Not tonight, Buddy," Cassidy said gently. "It's bed time." Eric's shoulders slumped. "We'll finish the tree tomorrow," she promised.

"All right," he said with resignation as he slowly went up the stairs.

"He's a good kid," Dylan said when Eric was out of earshot.

Cassidy smiled. "You of anyone know that he isn't always good, but most of the time he is pretty well behaved."

"I'm glad that he's anxious to help you out." Dylan sat down in a chair on the other side of the room, not wanting to mess up the bed that Eric had made on the couch.

"He has a protective streak when it comes to me." Her eyes were sad. "Unfortunately, I think part of that stems from what he remembers about his father."

"Some boys think that when their dad treats their mom that way that that's just how men treat women, and they grow up disrespecting and hurting women just like their fathers. I don't see that in Eric, though. I think he learned compassion and respect from you."

Cassidy smiled and blinked hard a few times. "I hope so."

They heard Eric thudding down the stairs. He ran into the living room and pushed a pile of clothing into Cassidy's arms. "I brought you your pajamas, Mom." Cassidy's face reddened, but she thanked Eric and tucked the wad under the blanket on the couch beside her. Dylan found her modesty and embarrassment endearing. He found his mind wandering to what her pajamas might look like for her to be embarrassed about them. Before he could let his imagination loose, Eric got his attention. He was grateful for the diversion.

"Will you come back tomorrow night to help finish decorating?" Eric looked at Dylan with his eyes widened, expectation etched in every line of his face. "You don't even have to bring Carlie if you don't want to. Mom always makes hot chocolate, lights the fire and plays Christmas music while we decorate. It's a lot of fun. You should come." All of his words ran together quickly in excitement.

"If it's okay with your mom, I'd be happy to join you." In fact, he would be disappointed to miss it. It sounded like the perfect way to spend an evening.

Eric let out a shout of victory. "It's okay with you, isn't it, Mom?"

"Yes," Cassidy said with a laugh. "Dylan would be very welcome to join us."

Eric ran over to her and gave her a hug and a kiss on the cheek, being careful to avoid bumping her ankle. "Thanks, Mom!" He stepped back and looked at her with concern. "I hope your ankle feels better soon. Can I get you anything else before I go to bed?"

Cassidy smiled at her son's grown up tone. "I think I'm good for now. Good night, sweetheart."

Cassidy and Dylan sat in silence as they listened to Eric climb the stairs one more time. They heard his door close and faintly heard the sound of his bed squeak as his weight hit it.

Cassidy looked over at Dylan. "He is a pretty good kid."

"I told you he was." Dylan scooted to the edge of his seat. "As fun as tonight has been – well, other than your ankle. . ." He stopped uncomfortably, cleared his throat, and shifted his eyes to his hands. How was he supposed to continue? He hated to add to her stress, but she needed to know about Hayley's visit to him. "I actually came here for another reason."

Cassidy's brows rose, but she kept quiet. Her fingers started tracing a pattern on the arm of her chair, and Dylan could tell that she was nervous about what was coming next.

He took a deep breath. "I had a visit today from Hayley Carter. She's one of the women who gave you a rough time at church yesterday." He looked up at Cassidy, and she nodded shortly to let him know she was listening. "Anyway, Hayley wanted me to know that there were going to be rumors about us – about me and you – because you came to lunch with me and Mom yesterday."

"And because you rescued me from her and her mom," Cassidy added.

Dylan rubbed the back of his neck awkwardly. "I wouldn't call it a rescue, but yeah, something like that." He met her eyes. "I just wanted you to know from me instead of hearing it from someone else."

"I appreciate that. I honestly don't think it will get far. People will know that someone like you wouldn't be with someone like me."

Dylan blinked. "Why wouldn't I want to be with someone like you?"

"Well, you know – I'm the single mom, the woman with a shady past, the prodigal child – you name it. And you're a good guy." Cassidy looked at him and shrugged. "It just doesn't add up."

Dylan crossed the room quickly. He perched on the arm of the couch near her and took her hand. "I don't agree with that at all. You're looking at it from the gossips' points of view, but not from my point of view. I don't see the rumors when I look at you, because I know the truth. Yes, you're a single mom and yes, you made some mistakes, but that's not who you are. You are a wonderful mom who cares about her child becoming a responsible adult. You are an intelligent rancher who has taken care of your grandfather's place and is turning it into what I'm sure will be a fantastic guest ranch. You are considerate, kind to my mother," he stroked her cheek gently, "and beautiful – inside and out." His eyes roamed her face before settling on her lips. He couldn't help himself. He leaned forward slowly, giving her plenty of opportunity to back away if she wanted. To his relief, she closed her eyes and moved towards him. He kissed her gently, sweetly, yet his heart still hammered in his chest. He sighed as he pulled back. "There is one way we could ruin the gossips' fun."

With her eyes still close, Cassidy murmured, "How?"

"We could make it true." He watched as her eyes flew open. "In fact, I think it's an excellent idea." He found himself holding his breath as he waited for her answer.

"What?" Her face was flushed, and he couldn't read her expression. "Are you serious?"

He traced her lips lightly with his finger. "I'm very serious." He leaned in to give her a quick kiss. "The more I get to know you, the more I want to spend time with you. I love being with both you and Eric. I'm so happy when we're together. Tonight was wonderful – except for your accident. I felt like we all belonged together, like we were family."

He heard her breathing quicken. Then she sighed. "I can't believe you felt it too."

Dylan laughed happily. "So what do you say? Wanna see where this could go?"

Cassidy closed her eyes and leaned her head back against the recliner. "The town is going to think you're crazy."

"I don't care what the town says or thinks. I know you, and I want to be with you." He held both of her hands. "Please say yes."

She opened her eyes and smiled. "I don't think I could possibly say no – because I feel the same way."

The Neighbor

Cassidy had just finished eating breakfast when the doorbell rang. She used the crutches to hobble to the door. She was surprised to see Jean standing there.

"Oh, my dear! Dylan told me you needed help today, because of your accident. I'm so sorry you're hurt." Jean patted a chair. "Let me take a look at your ankle." Unwrapping the ankle, she gently touched it. "It looks so swollen. Have you been icing it?"

"It actually looks better today than it did last evening. I haven't iced it yet today, but I have taken some ibuprofen," she admitted.

"I'll get you some ice. You keep your foot elevated." Jean bustled into the kitchen. Cassidy couldn't help, but smile. It had been so long since someone had mothered her that she decided to soak it up. It wasn't long before Jean came back and placed the ice on her ankle. "Now, you are going to rest today so anything you need, just let me know."

Cassidy laughed. "I haven't been this spoiled in a long time."

"Well, it's about time then." Jean brought over a pillow and put it behind Cassidy's back. Then she grabbed the remote and handed it to her. "Now, I'll just go finish cleaning up the breakfast dishes."

Cassidy shook her head, only feeling slightly guilty as

she turned on the television. There were no sick days or vacation days in ranching or mothering. It felt good to relax for once.

She didn't know when she fell asleep, but it was just before noon when the doorbell rang. She started to get up, but stopped when Jean bustled in.

"Don't get up," Jean said as she passed through. "I've got it."

A moment later, Warren Clifford came in. He took a seat on the couch, removing his hat as he did. He held his hat by the brim and began twisting in his hands nervously. "Sorry about your ankle, Ms. Golden. Mrs. Thompson told me you sprained it last night."

"Thanks. I'm sure I'll be back to normal in no time." Cassidy wondered why her neighbor was visiting. It was clear that he was uncomfortable, but she had no idea what he could be there for.

After a moment of awkward silence, Warren looked up at her and smiled sheepishly. "This shouldn't be difficult, but I don't want you to think I'm criticizing so I'm trying to frame my words carefully."

"I promise to understand that whatever you say is not meant to be critical," Cassidy assured him.

He smiled in relief. "I bought your tractor – one of your grandpa's antique ones. I felt like your asking price was fair, but when Rex delivered it, he asked for a pretty steep delivery fee."

Cassidy frowned. "There shouldn't have been any delivery fee. I could see charging one if we had to ship it across the country or something, but you're right next door. Do you have a receipt or a check or anything?"

Warren pulled a sheet from his back pocket. In Rex's handwriting was the agreement between the two ranchers, but added at the bottom was an extra fee. The ink was different and looked like it had been tagged on later.

Cassidy shook her head and pushed herself up from her chair, ignoring Jean's protests. She went to the office, motioning for Warren to follow her. Digging through the papers on her desk, she found her copy of the agreement. She wasn't surprised that there wasn't a delivery fee on her copy.

"I knew that I hadn't seen that fee. I'm so sorry." Cassidy looked up at Warren. "It seems like Rex may be trying to make a little extra off of my sales. Some of the other pieces I've sold off haven't seemed right either."

"I somehow felt like you may not have known about that transaction," Warren said. "Sorry he's been cheating you on other sales as well."

Cassidy felt anger rising up inside her. "Rex couldn't be so stupid to think that I'd never figure this out, could he?"

Warren chuckled. "Well, Rex has never been accused of being bright. He seems to have it in for you. I know for sure that he's behind at least a few of the rumors that have been spread about you."

"He thought that he would inherit the ranch when grandpa died. He thinks I've stolen it from under him."

Warren nodded as he followed her back into the living room. "Sounds about right."

"What should I do?" Cassidy couldn't remember asking any of her fellow ranchers for advice before, but she really had no idea how to proceed in this case.

Warren pursed his lips as he stood in front of the fireplace, hands in his pockets, rocking back on his heels. "I suppose getting rid of him isn't an option?"

Cassidy shook her head. "Grandpa put a stipulation in his will that he be given a job for life unless he did something terrible."

"Well, I'd say he's crossed that line," Warren pointed

out.

Cassidy shrugged. "Maybe, but I think it'd be hard to prove and with the way the town feels about me, there's a good chance I'd lose that lawsuit."

Warren nodded. "We need some absolute proof then." He scratched his chin, and Cassidy could hear the sandpaper scratch that it made. "The sheriff is a friend of mine. I'll talk to him and see what he thinks. I'll call him now since he'll probably want to talk to you as well." Jean came back in the room with a worried look on her face. She had a tray with mugs of coffee on it.

"I'm glad to see you back in your recliner! Dylan will kill me if anything else happens to you." Jean fussed over her as she got her situated.

"I just needed to check on something," Cassidy reassured her. "I'm fine."

Warren was on his phone, and she vaguely heard him talking as she tried to convince Jean that her brief excursion hadn't caused any further damage. Eventually, Warren handed her his phone. "Clyde just wants to ask you a few questions."

Cassidy felt her heart pound in her chest. She hoped that he didn't believe the things that had been spread about her. She grabbed the phone and put it to her ear. "Hello?"

"Hi, Ms. Golden. This is Clyde Robinson. Warren's been telling me about some strange things going on at Golden Creek Ranch. I just want to clarify a few things." His voice was warm, but professional, and Cassidy felt herself begin to relax.

"Of course. Ask away."

He asked a few questions about when everything took place, if she had noticed anything else suspicious, before he asked, "Has Rex Wilson done anything else to harm you before this? Or do you have suspicions that he has done anything else?"

Cassidy hesitated. "I have suspicions, but nothing tangible."

"Go ahead."

She sighed. "I think he may be responsible for the rumors that have plagued me since moving here."

"What makes you think that he is behind them?" The sheriff was friendly, but persistent.

She shifted in the recliner. "Well, mostly because they started after my grandfather passed away and the will was read. He left angry, yelling at me about being a gold digger and taking advantage of an old man. He didn't come home until late, and the following day was when I began to get treated differently in town. Eventually I heard many of the rumors." She shrugged even though she knew he couldn't see her through the phone. "It's certainly not evidence that would stand up in court, but it makes sense to me."

"If you don't trust Mr. Wilson, why do you keep him on?"

"Because according to my grandpa's will, I can't let him go unless he wants to leave, or he has caused some sort of damage. If I fire him, I can guarantee that he will sue and with only shaky evidence at best, I could lose everything." Cassidy was only partially aware of Jean and Warren's presence in the room. She knew that they were supporting her and there to help should she need it.

"That sounds like your grandpa," Clyde said, and Cassidy could swear that he was smiling. "Ray had a heart of gold, but sometimes he trusted people he shouldn't. Rex was an alcoholic rodeo clown when Ray found him. He got him back on his feet, but never could get him to completely stay away from drinking. He was able to get him to where he could at least function well enough to work during the day which was an improvement."

Cassidy smiled fondly. That sounded exactly like her grandpa. "I had never heard that story. Thank you."

"Anytime." Clyde hesitated a moment. "For what it's worth, Ms. Golden, I didn't believe the rumors, and I trust your intuition in this situation, but we're going to need more evidence."

"I understand. What would you like me to do?" Cassidy squared her shoulders, determined that she was going to handle this thing and get it behind her.

"I want you to go on as usual. Pretend like you don't know about the extra charges, like everything is normal. Rex needs to feel comfortable. Gather all of the recent receipts you have from sales and we'll track down the buyers and see if theirs match up. We'll take a look at Rex's account and see if recent deposits match up. I'll also see what we can find out around town. Rex sometimes lets things slip when he's been drinking. Maybe someone has heard something."

"Thank you so much!" Cassidy felt her eyes well as she thought about the support that she suddenly had from so many places. Maybe it was there all the time, she just couldn't see it because she was too busy building her island so she wouldn't get hurt.

"No problem. It's my job. Besides, your grandpa would have wanted us to protect his family." Clyde disconnected, and Cassidy felt relieved that someone else was helping her handle this problem. She looked up and saw Warren and Jean sitting on the couch, looking at her expectantly. She smiled. She had a whole crew of people who were standing beside her, helping her through this time.

"Well?" Jean asked expectantly. Cassidy had heard Warren talking with Jean while she was on the phone so she assumed that he had filled her in on what was going on.

"The sheriff is going to have the sales looked at and

check Rex's account. He is also going to ask around to see if Rex has talked to anyone about his plans. In the meantime, we're supposed to act like everything is normal."

Jean looked worried. She wrung her hands in her lap. "I don't like you being out here alone with this going on."

"I don't think Rex wants to physically harm me. He just wants what belongs to me. As long as I don't get in his way, I don't think he'd hurt me." The more she thought about it, the more the plan the sheriff laid out for her made sense. If Rex didn't suspect she knew, he would be more likely to relax, and if she stayed out of his way, there was no reason to harm her. Something like that would only cause him more problems. If he thought she knew something though, he could retaliate. No one wanted that.

"I still don't like it." Jean stood up and started pacing the room. "Maybe I should stay with you. With your hurt ankle, no one would think I was here for any other reason."

"Jean, you're going to be leaving soon to visit your sister. I don't want to put you out."

"It might not be a bad idea if Mrs. Thompson is willing," Warren spoke up. He rose from his place on the couch. "Having another set of eyes and ears about certainly wouldn't hurt anything." He placed his hat back on his head. "Well, I'd better head back to my place. If you need anything don't hesitate to call." He started for the door. "When you leave for your sister's place, let me know. Maybe my wife can stay with her if this thing isn't resolved by then."

"Warren, I don't think there's any need to put Karen out like that," Cassidy insisted.

"I'll let you know." Jean overrode Cassidy's decision neatly and emphatically. Warren nodded before he stepped outside. Jean turned back to Cassidy. "I'm not going to let you do this on your own."

"I noticed," Cassidy said wryly.

"Beside, Dylan wouldn't let me leave you alone even if I wanted to." Jean smiled warmly. "You have no idea how glad I am that he's finally found someone like you. I've prayed for you his whole life."

Cassidy's eyes widened. "We just . . . it's still early . . ." she sputtered.

"Oh I know. But even if it doesn't get to the point of being serious, maybe having you jolt him out of his single rut will get him to be looking around more." Jean leaned forward confidentially. "Between us though, I think you're 'the one'." She winked and headed towards the kitchen, leaving Cassidy behind, speechless.

The Phone Call

Dylan called his mom after getting back from lunch. He considered it a triumph that he hadn't called sooner. He had been thinking about Cassidy all day. When he had called his mom to ask her to take care of Cassidy, Jean had been concerned about Cassidy having to do all the ranch chores on her sprained ankle, but she had been overjoyed when he had explained that they had moved beyond friendship the night before. Dylan smiled recalling the squeal that his mom had let loose when he had told her.

Jean picked up after just a couple of rings. "How's she doing?" Dylan asked immediately. He wished he could be there to take care of Cassidy himself, but having his mom there was next best.

"She's resting right now. She slept most of the morning, too." She lowered her voice as if afraid Cassidy could hear her. "I think she needs the rest. Poor girl!"

Dylan smiled affectionately. His mom was in her element when there was someone to nurture. "How's everything else going?"

"Great! I gathered eggs and fed the chickens, then went down to the barn and took care of the horses. I helped with some of the house chores. Then I made her some lunch and now I'm doing laundry." The excitement in her voice was so clearly evident that he could picture her eyes sparkling.

"Sounds like you've been having fun playing on the ranch," he chuckled.

Jean laughed softly. "I guess so. It's been awhile since I've been able to do farm chores." She paused a moment. "I think you should know that Warren Clifford stopped by."

Dylan frowned for a moment in confusion. "Her neighbor? I take it that it wasn't a friendly call." He had thought highly of Warren. He hoped that he wasn't causing Cassidy any trouble.

"Well, in a way it was. You know that she's been selling some things in order to change Golden Creek Ranch into a guest ranch?" Dylan murmured in assent. "Well, apparently Warren bought a tractor from her, but Rex charged him a delivery fee that Cassidy didn't ask for."

"That explains some of the property that didn't get as much as she was expecting as well. So what is Cassidy going to do now?" Dylan ran his hand through his hair.

"Warren made her call the sherriff."

Dylan's eyes widened. Thoughts rushed through his head. If the sheriff believed the rumors about Cassidy this could be awkward. "What did he say?"

"He was very nice. He told her to act like everything was normal so Rex wouldn't get suspicious. He's going to be checking out the other sales and Rex's accounts and also ask around town to see if anyone knows anything." Jean hesitated again. "I decided that I'm going to stay here for a few days – either until I have to leave or until this is settled. Cassidy's sprain gives me a good excuse to be here. I just don't feel safe having her here alone."

Dylan breathed a sigh of relief. "That's a great idea. If you have to leave before it's settled," he started, but she was quick to interrupt him.

"Then Warren's wife will stay with her. He already offered, and I was so thankful that he jumped in with the offer. I wouldn't have felt right leaving to visit Paige if she had been left alone."

"I'm so glad that she's being protected. Hopefully this will be resolved soon." He drummed his fingers on the top of his desk. "Do you think I could speak with Cassidy?"

"Let me see if she's awake." He heard his mom's footsteps and then a murmur of voices before Cassidy's voice drifted over the line.

"Hey! How's your ankle doing?" He smiled just hearing her voice on the phone. He shook his head in amusement. He felt like a teenage boy with his first crush.

"Not as swollen, but still tender. Your mom has been a tremendous help."

"I'm glad. I was afraid you'd try to send her home," he admitted.

"I thought about it, but she didn't give me a chance," she said laughingly. "Once I sat down and elevated my foot though, I wouldn't have argued with her for the world. It just felt too good to relax."

"Good! You need some time to relax." He put his own boots up on his desk. "I hear you've had a bit of excitement."

"Yeah, it's been – interesting." Her voice trembled slightly belying the lightness she had tried to affect. "Sounds like my life may be under scrutiny even more."

"Well, yeah, but this time it's to help you, not hurt you," Dylan pointed out.

"I was so relieved when Sheriff Robinson believed me," she admitted. "I wasn't sure what he'd heard or what he thought about me." He heard the sound of her chair squeaking. "But Dylan, your mom doesn't need to stay with me," she said in a lowered voice. "I don't want to put her out."

"You aren't. She's excited to help out. It would be

135

worse for her if you didn't let her stay with you, because she'd be constantly worried." Dylan set his feet back on the floor. "Besides, it puts my mind at ease, too. I'd hate to think about you being there all alone – especially since the prime suspect is Rex."

"It's sweet that you're concerned about me." Her voice sounded dreamy, and he was glad to hear it so that he knew he wasn't the only one feeling that way.

"It's been too long since you've had someone concerned about you. I'm guessing the last time someone really cared about your well-being was when your grandpa was alive." Dylan tried to imagine a life where no one really cared about him, but it wouldn't surface.

"Well, Eric cares about me. He's just too young to take care of me. Does that make sense?"

Dylan smiled. "Perfectly. Give him time though, and I'll bet he'll take real good care of his mom."

"Just like you do." Dylan thought of how he had dropped everything to come take care of his mom after his dad had passed away. He'd do it all over again, though.

"Yeah, I guess so. It was all worth it. She did so much for me." He cleared his throat. "Eric's a good kid. He'll make you proud."

"He already does." He could picture the smile that she had on her face as she said it, a soft smile that spoke of the pride she had in her son. "I just hope that he becomes a godly man. I'm not sure that I've given him too much help in that area."

"We'll pray for him. Together we'll teach him what that looks like."

"Together," she sighed. "That's a lovely word. 'Alone' has fit my life so much better lately." He heard the chair squeak as she repositioned herself again. "By the way, Eric doesn't know that we are together yet. I didn't have a chance to tell him this morning, and I'd like to tell him when it's just the two of us."

Dylan got up and began to pace his office. "That's understandable, but it's going to be hard not to let it slip tonight while we're decorating the tree."

"I was thinking that if you could take your mom to her house to pick up her things, that would leave Eric and I alone for a little while, and I could talk to him then."

"But isn't my mom's car at your house? It might be difficult to explain why a grown woman needs her son to help her pack." Dylan stopped pacing and gazed sightlessly at the wall of photos.

"That's true," she said with concern. "Could you make some excuse to give us some time?"

Dylan smiled slowly. "Why don't you let me play ranch hand tonight? While mom goes to pick up her things, I'll do the evening chores, and you can use that time to tell Eric about us."

"That's a great idea. I'll let your mom know. She seems like the kind that will get it done before you get here in her eagerness to help out."

Dylan laughed. "You're probably right. That sounds just like her." He headed back for his desk. As he sat down in the old chair and leaned back, he asked, "So what happens if Eric isn't happy about us?"

For a while he couldn't hear anything, but her breathing. He knew that she was thinking his question through seriously. Finally, he heard her sigh. "I don't know. I think we would need to take a step back and hope that one day he feels comfortable with the idea. I can't put my love life above his comfort."

"No good mom would," Dylan agreed.

"Honestly though, I can't see him being unhappy with the situation." She chuckled. "After all, you bring Carlie into the picture."

Dylan laughed heartily. "You're probably right. I should get back to work, but I'm looking forward to seeing you tonight."

"I'm looking forward to it, too. Good-bye."

Dylan slowly lowered his phone to his desk. He knew he had an idiotic grin on his face, but he didn't care. Tonight he would get to be part of the Golden family, and he just couldn't wait.

The Change of Plans

Rex was fixing a fence when he saw a woman walking towards him. He groaned thinking that Cassidy was coming, most likely to check up on him or ask more probing questions about the sales he had made. Maybe she was just bored of sitting in the office and staring at the walls. But Rex had seen Warren Clifford come to the house earlier and it had made him edgy. After all, he hadn't told Cassidy about the "delivery fee" that he had charged their neighbor.

Rex looked over his shoulder again and realized that the woman wasn't Cassidy. It was an older lady, one who looked vaguely familiar. He racked his brain trying to come up with her name. Johnson? Thomas? Thompson! That's it! The lady who owned the feed store. His brow furrowed in confusion. What was she doing out here? More importantly, why was she seeking him out? There was nothing else to bring her all the way out to this part of the property. He wiped his hands on his jeans and stood up. He watched her warily as she approached, but he saw only friendliness on her face.

"Hi, Mr. Wilson," she greeted him as she neared. "Cassidy told me I might find you here."

"Mrs. Thompson. This is a surprise. What can I do for you?"

Jean pulled her coat tighter around herself as the wind blew over them. Her hair fluttered around her face for a moment before settling back into its normal place. "I just wanted to let you know that Cassidy sprained her ankle last night while getting Christmas decorations from the shed. I'm moving in for a while to help her out."

Rex knew he should show some sympathy, but felt elation grow in his chest instead. He schooled his features. "Well, now, that's too bad. I hope she's not in a lot of pain."

"As long as she keeps off that foot, she's feeling all right. It's a pretty bad sprain though. She may be laid up until after Christmas." Jean shook her head sadly. "I'm going to visit my sister in Arizona for Christmas, but if she's still not feeling well by then, Karen Clifford said that she would come and stay with Cassidy, so tell Mae that she doesn't need to have Cassidy on her mind."

Rex narrowed his eyes. Did she really think that Mae would take care of Cassidy, or was she getting in a dig? He decided to play along in either case. "I'll let her know."

"Thanks! I'm going to do Cassidy's chores, and she can still do the office work so it shouldn't add any more work for you."

"I appreciate that."

"Well, I better get back to Cassidy. I just thought you ought to know." Jean gave a little smile and turned to walk back towards the house. Rex watched her go, his brow furrowed. What was that all about? He sensed an undercurrent, but couldn't place his finger on what it was.

Suddenly, his lips began to widen. He threw his head back and laughed. He no longer needed to wait for the storm that may or may not come. Cassidy was laid up, and that Thompson woman wouldn't know if his behavior was normal or not. He could rob her blind – uh – take what was rightfully his. He couldn't wait to tell Mae.

He burst through the front door and ran over to Mae. He grabbed her hands and pulled her up from the couch. Swinging her around, he lowered her into a dip and kissed her in a manner that he hadn't done for years. When he released her, Mae stared up at him in wonder.

"Wow. Where did that come from?" she breathed.

"Things are looking up! Guess what I found out?"

"I can't imagine," Mae answered dryly. Clearly she had determined that he was setting himself up to fail again.

"Cassidy sprained her ankle and is laid up, maybe even until after Christmas. She's got the Thompson woman staying with her to help out, possibly Clifford's wife as well. She's defenseless, and no one will see it coming. By the time they figure it out, we'll be safely gone."

Mae brightened. "Oh, maybe your crazy plan will work after all."

Rex scowled. "Crazy plan? My crazy plan? That's what you think?"

Mae sat back down on the couch. "Well, Rex, you do a lot of big talking, but not a lot of doing. I didn't think you'd actually go through with it."

Rex put his hands on his hips. "I'll show you. Someday, you'll be proud to be married to me."

Mae snorted. "On that day, I will call my mother and tell her she was wrong to say all those nasty things about you."

Rex grinned. "Oh yes you will. And then she'll apologize to me personally."

He was leaving the room when he heard her mutter under her breath. "I wouldn't hold my breath."

******

Cassidy heard Jean come back into the house. She had said that she had a quick chore to do and disappeared for a

141

while. She wondered what Jean had been up to, especially when she heard her talking excitedly on the phone just after she came back in.

In a short time, Jean's light step could be heard, and she entered the living room. "How are you, dear?" She began tidying up around the living room, picking up Cassidy's dishes from lunch, straightening the pillows on the couch.

"I'm fine," Cassidy answered curiously. "You seem like you're excited about something. What's going on?"

Jean sat down on the couch near Cassidy's recliner. Her face shone with eagerness, and her hands clenched in excitement. "I think we may be near the end of your mystery."

Cassidy raised her eyebrows. "Oh? What makes you think that? We just got started on it."

"I may have set something in motion." Jean reminded Cassidy of when Eric was excited about getting a blue ribbon at school for a project he had completed. But Cassidy worried about what Jean may have done. She didn't want Dylan's mom getting into the middle of everything and possibly setting herself up as a target. Although she supposed that Jean was already involved since she was staying in her house.

"What did you do?" Cassidy asked warily.

"I had a conversation with Rex." Jean sat back on the couch smugly, folding her arms across her chest.

"About what?" Cassidy felt her heart sink. She really hoped that Jean hadn't complicated things.

"I let him know that you're hurt and that I'll be staying with you for a while. I hinted that you may be laid up until after Christmas."

Cassidy's brow furrowed. "Why? What does that accomplish?"

"Don't you see?" Jean leaned forward again in

142

eagerness. "If Rex thinks that someone who is unfamiliar with Golden Creek Ranch and its workings is the only one who may see him make his next move, he'll be more likely to go through with it – and quickly, because he'll want to get it done before you get back up on your feet."

Cassidy thought it over and slowly nodded. "That's actually a great idea."

Jean beamed at her. "That's what the sheriff said, too, when I called him to let him know. He's going to make sure that if Rex moves, someone is going to see him do it."

Cassidy shook her head. "I never thought I'd be involved in something like this. I just wanted a quiet life when I moved to the ranch."

Jean patted her leg gently. "I know. But we're here to help you through this, and hopefully it will be done with before Christmas, and we can forget all about it." Jean stood up and was about to leave the room when she turned around. "Would you like me to ask my pastor to be praying for this situation?"

Cassidy started to shake her head, but then stopped. "You know, it certainly wouldn't hurt to have some Divine intervention here, but in a small town like this, I'm afraid that it will start getting around town."

Jean leaned against the wall. "I could tell him that I can't tell him all the details, but that there's a situation I'd like him to pray about."

Cassidy nodded slowly. "That would probably work." She looked at Jean worriedly. "Do you think that will be enough information for God?"

Jean smiled affectionately. "Oh, honey. God already knows the intricate details of what is going on here. He already knows how it will end."

"Then why pray? If He already knows what's going to happen, then why pray about it?"

"I can't explain it all, but I know that the Bible tells of times when people prayed, and God answered. King Hezekiah was told he was going to die, but when he prayed, God gave him a longer life. Besides that, the Bible says that there is power in the prayer of people agreeing together." Jean shrugged. "It's one of the mysteries of the Christian life, but I think God likes for us to talk to Him, just like you like for Eric to come to you when he has a problem."

Cassidy frowned. It was so confusing. Yet she felt drawn to Jean's suggestion. "Go ahead and ask him, but please be discreet."

Jean smiled. "You've got it." She stood upright and headed out of the room. Over her shoulder she said, "You may want to get used to playing the invalid. I wouldn't be surprised if Rex stops by to make sure my story is true. It won't do to have him see you walking around the ranch either so I'm afraid you're homebound for a while."

Cassidy groaned. She couldn't wait until this mess was done.

The Tree Decorating

Cassidy was hobbling back to her recliner on her crutches when she heard Dylan's truck pull up. Funny how she could already distinguish the sound of his truck from other vehicles. She eased herself back into the chair and put her feet up. Already she felt better. Tomorrow she was sure that she could be more help around the house. She knew that Jean was right and that she was going to be homebound until after Christmas, but she hoped that moving around the rooms of her house would keep her from losing her sanity.

The door slammed open and Eric ran in with Carlie on his heels. Jean peeked her head in from the kitchen. "I'm going to head home now to grab my things. Dinner is in the oven and should be ready by the time I'm back."

"All right. Thanks, Jean." Cassidy heard her speak to Dylan on the porch before she got in her car and left.

Eric came over and gave his mom a kiss. He sat on the arm of the recliner and rested his head on top of hers. Cassidy closed her eyes, enjoying the moment. More and more Eric was uncomfortable with showing affection for her. She knew that her injury had brought out a protective side in her son.

"Why is Mrs. Thompson getting her things?" he asked.

"She's going to stay here with us to help out while my ankle heals up." Cassidy wondered how much she would have to explain to Eric about the situation. She prayed that he wouldn't need further details. He could either get nervous or give information away unintentionally and make things worse.

"I can take care of you!" He pulled away from his mom and pulled the afghan over the top of her as if to prove that he was competent to handle the nursing duties. She was so touched by his care that she didn't have the heart to tell him that she was roasting as it was.

"Honey, I know you can, but you have school, and then you're helping out at the feed store. This way I have someone to help me all day. Plus there are things you can't help me with."

"Like what?" He folded her arms across his chest protectively.

"Like girl stuff," Cassidy said with a lowered voice.

"Oh gross, Mom!" Cassidy smiled. She knew that simple phrase would work wonders in getting Eric to realize that he couldn't do it all. "I guess it might be nice to have her here."

"Well, don't sound so enthusiastic when she gets back, or you might overwhelm her," Cassidy said dryly.

Eric smirked. "Aw, Mom. You know I'll be good for her." He stood up and grabbed his backpack.

"Before you leave, I have one other thing to talk to you about." Eric watched her warily as he moved to the couch.

"Okay," he drawled out slowly.

"Last night after you went to bed, Dylan and I got to talking, and we'd like to, sort of, be a couple." Cassidy held her breath as waited for Eric's response.

He let out his breath loudly. "Geez, Mom! That's it? You scared me half to death!"

"So you don't mind?" Cassidy wanted to make sure that Eric understood what he would be agreeing to.

"Mom." The tone of his voice told her that he thought

her question was stupid. "Why would I mind? Dylan's a good guy and he likes you – like, likes likes you. Plus if things work out with you guys, then I get to have Carlie back." He smiled broadly and winked at his mom. Carlie heard her name and came over to Eric's side. He rubbed her ears, and she leaned into him.

Cassidy smiled as she watched the two of them together. "You've thought this all out, huh?"

Eric shrugged. "I thought it might be a possibility. Dylan's like the most opposite from Dad you could get. I trust him, and I like him. I don't think it'd be so bad to have him around more."

"Especially if he brings Carlie with him?" Cassidy teased him.

Eric stood up and slung his backpack over his shoulder. For a moment, Cassidy saw the young man he was becoming. She blinked and her young son was back. "Even if it's just Dylan, I like having him around." He left the room and headed up the stairs. Carlie looked between Cassidy and Eric for a moment. She licked Cassidy's hand almost in apology and then followed Eric up the stairs.

Cassidy smiled in contentment. Eric had easily accepted their new relationship status. Yet, he didn't seem as if his world would collapse if she and Dylan didn't end up together. Not yet anyway. She knew the longer they were together, the harder it would be for all of them if it didn't work out.

"Lord, if this isn't what You want for us, please end it quickly before we get too deep. I don't want any of us to get hurt."

The kitchen door opened, and Cassidy heard the faucet at the sink turn on. Dylan had finished with the chores and was washing up. She smiled at how natural it felt to have him help, to have him with her. She heard his boots as he crossed the floor. As he entered the living room, she looked up at him with a large smile.

"Hey," she said shyly.

"Hey. How are you feeling?" He spoke softly as he moved closer to her.

"I'm wonderful." She knew her grin was bordering on idiotic, but she couldn't help herself.

He laughed. "You're wonderful with a sprained ankle, mysterious events happening, and the police watching your ranch?"

"I'm wonderful, because you're here."

Dylan's voice was rough with emotion as he leaned in towards her. "That's funny, because I'm wonderful because I'm here, too." He pressed his lips against hers and then pulled back. He kneeled beside her chair, almost as if he couldn't bear to be separated any further than that from her. "I take it your talk with Eric went well?"

"He thinks you like like me," she answered with a smile.

"Does he? He's right. How about you? Do you like like me?"

"I do." Cassidy startled at the sound of those words - the words that had so much meaning in a wedding ceremony. She watched him carefully to see if he had picked up on it as well, but he only smiled.

"That's a very good thing." He leaned in again to kiss her, and both of them were so immersed in their own world, that they missed the sound of Eric's footsteps on the stairs.

"Oh, gross!" His disgusted words broke them apart quickly, but they quickly dissolved into giggles. "If you're going to be doing that all the time, then I'm not sure this is going to work out."

Dylan stood to his feet and pulled Eric against him. "Maybe you can start clearing your throat when you enter a room."

Eric scoffed. "It's not like I tiptoed down the stairs." They heard the sound of wheels on gravel. "Mrs. Thompson must be back. I'll go see if she needs any help." He rushed out of the room, but hollered over his shoulder, "No more mushy stuff!"

Dylan laughed and moved to the couch. "I better sit over here if we're not allowed to do any mushy stuff."

"Distance might be beneficial for now," Cassidy agreed. She sobered. "While Eric's gone, did your mom tell you what she did?"

Dylan looked confused. "What do you mean?"

Cassidy quickly explained how Jean had let Rex know about her accident and had basically given him the green light to proceed with any plans he might have. "She felt like if he knew I wouldn't see him do it, he might act more quickly and then we'd be done with this mess."

"I think that just might work," Dylan responded.

"The sheriff thought so, too. They're making sure there are eyes on Rex at all times for a while." The kitchen door opened, and they heard Eric and Jean talking as they entered.

"And then I came downstairs and they were kissing!" Eric put all the horror he could muster into the last word.

"Well, I suppose that might be happening more frequently for now," Jean comforted him. "I think we're just going to have to get used to it."

Dylan and Cassidy exchanged smiles. Eric might second guess his approval of their relationship if he caught them kissing often.

"I don't want to get used to it. It makes me sick." Cassidy and Dylan laughed heartily.

"I guess we'll have to keep public displays of affection to a minimum when Eric's around," Dylan said.

"I guess so. Are you okay with that?" Cassidy asked worriedly.

Dylan grasped her hand lovingly. "I want to be with you, but I want Eric to be comfortable with it, too. If that means not being physically affectionate, then I can deal with that."

"We're coming in now!" Eric hollered making the couple chuckle again. Jean followed Eric into the room.

"Dinner is on the table," Jean announced. "Do you think you can make it, Cassidy?"

"I'll be fine," Cassidy assured her. Dylan helped her out of the recliner and got her crutches for her, but he allowed her to make her own way to the table. It made Cassidy love him more. He cared for her, but didn't smother her.

Love? Cassidy glanced quickly at Dylan. As she watched him, she realized that somewhere along the way she had fallen in love with him. He was attractive, sure, but it was more than that. She loved that he saw past the rumors to see her. She loved that he didn't see Eric as a nuisance, but genuinely cared for him. She loved that he had left behind his own ambitions to care for his mom when his dad had passed away. She loved that he was a Christian and wanted to please God. She wondered if she dared tell him how she felt.

Cassidy was quiet over dinner. Her mind was stuck on her newfound understanding of her feelings for Dylan. If anyone noticed, they didn't say anything. She figured that with the events occurring on the ranch and her sprained ankle, they probably thought she was just a bit overwhelmed.

It was while Jean and Dylan were cleaning up that there was a knock at the door. Dylan dried his hands before answering the door. Rex and Mae stood side by side wearing awkward smiles.

"We heard Ms. Golden had been injured and just wanted to stop by and see if she needed anything," Rex explained.

"I brought a pie," Mae added.

Dylan stepped aside and let the couple in. Cassidy saw Dylan and Jean exchange a secretive smile. It hadn't taken long for the couple to make sure the story was true.

Cassidy welcomed the couple with a smile. "Please make yourself at home," she said. Her own leg was propped up on another chair at the table. "It's so nice of you to stop by."

"Here you go, Mom," Eric said coming into the room. "Here's your ice pack and the ibuprofen." He handed the objects to his mom before he greeted their guests. "I'm going to go play with Carlie unless you need something else." The pleading in his eyes clearly showed how much he hoped there was nothing else for him to do.

"That's fine. Thank you for helping." Cassidy watched her son bound out of the room. Jean brought over a glass of water for her to take the medicine. She then gently placed the ice pack on her ankle before returning to the sink to finish up the dishes.

"Looks like you've got plenty of help," Rex said.

"I'm very blessed. Between you running things so smoothly outside and Jean taking such good care of me inside, I'm being spoiled." Cassidy smiled warmly, but internally she hoped that her kind words made Rex squirm.

"Well, your grandpa was so good to me that it's only right that I care for his family as much as I can." Cassidy wanted to gag. She couldn't believe how brazen he was.

"I brought a pie," Mae reiterated, pushing the box across the table. The store bought pie could be seen through the plastic window in the box. The gooey apple filling peeked through the crust and large sugar crystals decorated

151

the crust.

"That was very thoughtful of you. Thank you!" Jean came back over and took the pie.

"I'll go cut everyone a piece," she said. "I don't want Cassidy to get up."

"I think there's some vanilla ice cream in the freezer," Cassidy mentioned as Jean took the pie to the counter.

"Would you like me to take a look at your ankle?" Rex asked. "I've had a sprain or two in my day. I can recognize the signs."

Cassidy exchanged glances with Jean and Dylan. Rex was being very thorough in making sure that she was actually hurt. Cassidy removed the ice pack and put her other foot near the swollen ankle so he could see the difference. Rex eagerly moved closer. He bent down low to study the two ankles.

"That does seem like it's a bad one. Has the swelling gone down?" He looked satisfied as she nodded. "I'd say that you should rest until at least Christmas. You don't want to overdo and end up re-injuring it. Just relax and take it easy. I'll take care of the ranch. Don't even have it on your mind."

"I think you're probably right. I'm so grateful for all the help I have." Cassidy placed the ice pack back on her ankle. Dylan placed a plate of pie with ice cream in front of her and then Mae.

Mae reached for the fork, but Rex grabbed her hand. "We should let you guys eat your dessert in peace. We just wanted to make sure that you're being cared for."

"There's no need to rush off," Cassidy insisted. "You're more than welcome to stay for some pie."

"Nah, we've stayed long enough." Mae glared at Rex then defiantly scooped a big bite of the pie in her mouth before he pulled her away. She mumbled a good-bye around the bite in her mouth as Rex shoved her out the door.

Cassidy waited a few moments before turning her attention back to Jean and Dylan. "Just wanted to make sure I'm being cared for," Cassidy parroted. "More like just wanted to be sure that I needed to be cared for."

"I nearly died when he asked to see your ankle," Jean said chuckling. "So obvious!"

"Poor Mae didn't even get to taste her pie," Dylan added as he cleaned her place.

Cassidy giggled. "They're quite a pair." She removed the ice pack once more and pushed herself to her feet. "Wasn't it great timing that Eric was getting me the ice and medicine?"

"It was perfectly divine timing," Jean agreed. "Definitely a God thing."

Cassidy used her crutches to go into the living room. Dylan followed closely. As soon as Eric saw them enter, he sprang to his feet. "Is it time?" he asked joyfully. Cassidy nodded and soon the room was bustling. Dylan laid a fire in the fireplace, and Eric got out the tree ornaments. Christmas music was playing from the stereo, and Jean came in from the kitchen carrying a tray of hot chocolate and cookies.

As Cassidy watched her son decorate the tree, her heart filled with love for the people in her life. Eric eagerly showed Dylan his favorite ornaments while Jean made sure they were all evenly spread out. Carlie lay warming herself by the fire. Cassidy wrapped her hands around her mug of cocoa and sighed. She finally had a family.

The Storm

The week of Christmas finally arrived. Jean was packing her bags to go visit her sister while Cassidy stood staring out the window. Nothing had happened yet with Rex. She supposed that gathering enough evidence took time, but with her ankle healed, Cassidy was growing increasingly restless. She longed to get outside, but several people had counseled her to stay in until Rex made his move – including the sheriff. That was probably what had made the biggest impact on her. Clyde had been sympathetic, but had maintained that Rex was more likely to act if she were still laid up.

Jean stepped out of the guest room with her bags. Her eyes filled with tears. "I don't want to leave you like this," she said. "I could still cancel my flight."

"Don't you even think about it!" Cassidy responded. "You would be disappointed if you missed your trip. Your sister is looking forward to seeing you."

"I'm going to miss all the excitement." Cassidy's lips twitched at the tone that so reminded her of Eric when he didn't get his way. All Jean needed was to cross her arms over her chest and a pout to make the image complete.

"We'll keep you up to date."

"It's not the same as being here." Jean sighed. "But I guess I had better go." She walked to stand next to Cassidy.

"Looks like that big snowstorm they've been promising for weeks is finally going to come."

The sky was gray with thick clouds, and the wind was blowing fiercely already. Dylan had made sure that she was prepared in case this storm became the blizzard that was predicted. It was nice to have someone who cared about her wellbeing again. "I guess we'll have our white Christmas after all."

"I won't. Arizona isn't known for having snow." Jean looked at Cassidy worriedly. "Will you be okay with the storm coming?"

"Dylan's made sure that I have all the supplies I'll need in case we're stuck here for a while or lose power. I'm sure we'll be fine."

Jean looked down the road. "I hope Karen Clifford makes it over before the storm rolls in. I don't want you to be alone."

"Now that I'm on my feet again, it won't be a big deal if she doesn't get over here in time. With the storm coming, Rex won't suspect that I'm back on my feet, just that she couldn't make it." Cassidy really wasn't concerned about being alone.

"But you'll be susceptible. If he thinks you know something, he may put you out of the way," Jean whispered eerily.

"Well, that's a cheery thought. I think you've been watching too many police dramas. I'm going to trust that Rex still thinks that we are not suspicious of him at all so he has no reason to 'put me out of the way'." Cassidy checked her watch. "You should get going, or you're going to miss your flight.

"All right," Jean said begrudgingly. She gave Cassidy a tight hug. "Take care of yourself."

"I will. Merry Christmas, Jean." She stepped back, and

Jean went to gather her suitcase and carry on bag.

Jean looked at her affectionately. "I'm glad Dylan has you to spend Christmas with. I would hate for him to be alone."

"I'm glad that Eric and I will have him, too. We've had some lonely Christmases since my grandpa died."

Jean smiled and headed to her car. Cassidy watched as she drove away. As she stood there the first flakes of snow began to fall. She turned back to the living room. The tree was lit and decorated in the corner. Presents were underneath neatly wrapped. A nativity held a place of honor on the mantle along with a stocking for Eric. With the snow falling outside the window, it finally felt like Christmas. Cassidy put on some Christmas music before heading to the office. At least she was able to do that work even if she was still trapped inside.

Rex hadn't been by to check on her again, but he asked Jean about her nearly every day. Clyde had told her that they had watched Rex and Mae begin to box their house up as if they were moving, but as of yet they hadn't seen them do anything illegal. Cassidy fully expected something to happen that day. It would be the perfect time. Jean was gone. Karen hadn't arrived. As far as Rex knew, Cassidy was still housebound with her ankle. A storm was coming to obliterate all traces and slow any pursuit. Today would be the perfect day for him to go through with his plan.

Cassidy took a moment to pray for the safety of all involved. As peaceful as the world seemed right now, a storm was coming.

******

Rex was pleased. He couldn't have asked for a better day for the Thompson woman to leave. The snow was coming more heavily. It would make things a bit more difficult, but it was still manageable yet. He'd be long gone by the time the blizzard fully hit. With Cassidy stuck at home alone, this should be easy.

He had parked the moving truck at the back of the little house, and they had been loading up all morning. Mae was surprisingly helpful. He figured she was just glad to finally be doing something. She kept up a steady stream of chatter about where they might end up and the properties she'd been looking at online. He hoped they ended up with enough to get one of the places she was looking at. They sounded perfect: lots of land, big house – and far away from Snowfall, Wyoming.

He had just put the last item in the truck when he heard the sound of a vehicle coming up the drive. His heart pounded excitedly. This was it. A large semi with a cattle car attached made its way towards the barn. Rex glanced nervously at the big house, hoping that Cassidy hadn't seen or heard the truck. He tried to think of what he would say if she had heard it. Then he decided that he had always been a quick thinker. He'd get out of it somehow.

He hurried over to the driver of the semi. "You're right on time," Rex said happily.

"Of course I am," the driver said, taking offense. "I'm always on time."

"Of course," Rex said. "I'll go ahead and gather the cattle up if you'll let down the ramp."

"I have done this before, you know," the trucker said with disdain.

Rex was too pleased with himself to take offense. He led the cows out to put on the truck. It was a lot more work by himself. Normally he'd have a few high school boys come help him. But this was a job that he needed to do alone. The more people that knew about it, the more likely he was to get caught. He was a little disgruntled that the truck driver didn't offer to help, but maybe it was better this way. He'd probably want more money for the extra help, and his service was already putting a dent in Rex's finances.

The blizzard was getting serious as he loaded the final cow onto the truck. "Mister, are you sure about this?" the driver asked. "This snow is getting thick."

"Well, then, you should get going now," Rex retorted.

The driver grumbled under his breath. Rex heard a comment about hazard pay, but he ignored it as he hurried back to the house.

"What are you doing, Rex?" Rex stopped suddenly. He had forgotten the boy. Eric had been working at the feed store so often that he hadn't expected him to be around. He cursed under his breath before turning around.

"What are you doing home? I thought you were helping out at Thompson's Feed," Rex growled.

"I normally do, but today Dylan sent me home early because of the storm coming."

"So you decided to spend time spying on me?"

Eric shrugged. "I'm just curious. I heard the truck come up, and saw you load it up with the cows. It's not the normal time to send them to auction, so I wondered what was going on."

Rex's mind raced. How was he going to get out of this? He didn't want to kill the kid although it definitely crossed his mind. Yet, he couldn't have the kid running and telling his mom. Maybe he could distract him. "Dylan Thompson's been hanging around your house a lot lately."

Eric grinned. "He's dating my mom. They can get mushy, but he brings Carlie with him so I don't mind."

Rex scratched his chin. "Must be hard for them with a kid around."

Eric's grin faded. "What do you mean?"

Rex shrugged. "Well, I know when I was dating a

woman I sure didn't want a kid hanging around. Gets in the way of romance." He lifted his eyebrows suggestively. "Won't be long before Dylan gets tired of it and leaves." He started to walk away. His plan had worked. Eric was no longer thinking about the truck or the cows.

"What should I do?" Eric asked as he scrambled after Rex.

He rolled his eyes with his back still to Eric. Maybe it hadn't worked. He turned around. "I'd lay low. Stay out of the way. Make them feel like you aren't even around."

"I can do that."

Rex smiled thinly. "Why don't you go try it out now? Go see if you can make yourself practically invisible." Rex chuckled as Eric ran off. Kids were so stupid. The wind gusted around him, making him shiver. He needed to get on the road if this was going to work. Ducking his head, he pushed against the wind and ran to the moving truck.

The Panic

The phone in the office rang as Cassidy was working on the ledgers on the computer. She quickly answered, but her mind was still on the numbers on the screen. There were so many items that didn't add up. When she recognized Clyde's voice, she immediately turned all her attention to the phone call.

"What's going on?" she asked eagerly.

"We've got some movement," the sheriff answered vaguely. "I don't want to get your hopes up too high, but I also want to encourage you to stay inside. You might want to keep your son out of the way, too."

"Eric shouldn't be going out in this storm anyway. I'll double check and make sure that he stays put though." Cassidy breathed a sigh of relief. She was so tired of being locked up in her own home. "Thank you so much!"

"Don't thank me quite yet," he cautioned. "You never know what might happen when people get desperate."

Cassidy set the phone down on the desk thoughtfully. Clyde hadn't seemed confident that this was over. She took a moment and prayed for the safety of all involved, and that it would be wrapped up that day. She was tired of living on eggshells.

Cassidy shoved herself out of the office chair and climbed up the stairs to find Eric. She tapped lightly on his door, but there was no answer. She wondered if he had fallen asleep. She knew he had come home already. Dylan hadn't wanted him to be caught in the storm so he had him come home, but had sent Carlie with him so that he wouldn't miss the opportunity to spend time with the dog. Softly she opened the door and peeked inside. Carlie pushed past her eagerly and tore down the stairs. Cassidy looked inside the room, but didn't see anyone.

Carlie came back to the bottom of the stairs and barked once, then hurried to the door. "I'm coming. Did Eric leave you in his room too long? Poor dog." As she opened the door, Carlie shoved past her and took off running through the heavy falling snow. Cassidy frowned and called her name, but with the wind howling, her voice came back to her. Great! Now she'd lost Dylan's dog. Both Eric and Dylan would be upset if anything happened to her. She was about to put on her boots and go looking for her when she remembered the sheriff's warning to stay inside. "Lord, keep her safe," she whispered. She felt terrible about leaving Carlie out there, but it was more important that she find Eric right now.

She searched the house from top to bottom. She even checked in the attic although she knew the room frightened her son. She felt the panic rising in her throat, churning her stomach. If Eric wasn't in the house, where was he?

She grabbed her coat and pulled on her boots. Sheriff or no sheriff, she needed to find her son. Stepping out onto the porch, she looked around trying to see some sign of life. The snow blustering around her made it impossible to see further than a few feet in front of her. She decided to check the barn, her pulse screaming at her to hurry. The door took all of her strength to open against the wind. She stepped inside to the warmth and looked around. The horses were shifting nervously. The storm had put them all on edge. She peered in each stall hoping to find Eric curled in a corner with a book or sleeping. Her brain knew she wasn't likely to find him there, but her heart longed to see his figure. Vaguely she noticed that Rex's horse wasn't in his stall, but worry about Eric forced that tidbit to the back of her mind.

Cassidy's heart pounded uncontrollably. She pulled her phone out of her back pocket and dialed the sheriff's number. "My son is missing!"

"Calm down, Ms. Golden." Clyde's soothing voice washed over her. "Are you sure he's gone?"

"I've looked everywhere. I can't find him. It'd be so easy to get lost in this storm." The sobs tore out of her throat, unable to hold them back any longer. The tears poured down her face as she thought of all the horrendous things that could have happened to Eric. It was her worst nightmare come true.

"All right. I'm sending a man out to your place, and I'll send an alert out to all my officers and the surrounding communities. I need you to do something for me though."

"What? I'll do anything!" Cassidy pressed the phone tightly to her ear.

"I need you to stay put. I know you'll want to go out looking for him. I know this is the toughest thing I could ask of you. But if you go wandering off, then I have two people to look for instead of one. Besides, he may come home while we're looking, and he'll need you to be there when he walks in. Can you do that for me?"

Cassidy nodded fervently before realizing that he couldn't see her. "Yes," she choked. "I'll stay at the house."

"Okay, good. I'll check in every once in a while, and if Eric does come home, you let me know." The sheriff's calm demeanor helped lower her heart rate, but the tears still flowed.

She hurried back to the house and made a quick check

through the rooms to make sure that he hadn't returned while she was out at the barn. The silence in the house was haunting. She sat at the kitchen table and buried her hands in her arms, sobbing uncontrollably. When she calmed a little, she lifted up a prayer, but all she could say was, "Please, please, God." She repeated the phrase over and over, thankful that the Spirit would translate the groaning of her heart. No other words formed.

She was so preoccupied that she didn't hear the footsteps on the porch or the door opening. A hand gripped her shoulder and she started. She looked up hopefully, then launched herself out of her chair and into Dylan's waiting arms.

"He's missing," she sobbed. "I don't know where he is. Where is he?"

Dylan rubbed her back gently. "Who's missing? What happened?" His voice was pitched low to help comfort and calm her.

"Eric!" Cassidy's voice rose hysterically, refusing to be calmed by him. "He's not here. I don't know where he went. Why would he leave? Why?"

Shock crossed Dylan's face. "You're sure he's not here? I had Warren bring him straight here well ahead of the storm!" He released her and began to tear through the house calling Eric's name.

Cassidy followed assuring Dylan that she had already searched the whole house, but deep down hoping that he knew of a spot that Eric might be tucked away that she hadn't thought of checking. After a thorough look, they knew that Eric was not in the house. There were no more places where they might have missed him.

Dylan stood in the middle of the kitchen with his hands on his hips. His forehead was drawn with worry. Cassidy slumped in a chair at the kitchen table, her head in her hands. She kept whispering desperate prayers.

"Nothing happened? You guys didn't fight or anything?" Dylan asked in confusion. "It doesn't make sense."

Cassidy shook her head. "I got word that Rex was making his move, and that Eric and I should stay in the house. I thought he was in his room so I went to tell him that we needed to stay put for a while, but he wasn't there. Carlie pushed past me, and I thought she needed to go outside, but when I opened the door, she took off running." Cassidy stopped and looked up at Dylan with wide eyes. "Oh, Dylan! I've been so concerned about Eric, I forgot to tell you about your dog. I'm so sorry."

Dylan waved it off. "That's understandable. We'll find Carlie." He came over and sat next to her. "Do you think Rex could have had anything to do with Eric's leaving?"

"Kidnapped?" Cassidy thought about it for a moment. "No. There's no reason for Rex to take him, and he always thought of Eric as a nuisance. Why would he take him?"

"Maybe Eric saw him," Dylan suggested softly.

Cassidy's face drained of color. "If Rex thought Eric was a threat, he might do something terrible to him." Even in her mind she couldn't spell out the details of what that might mean. Her heart sank at the idea of her son being in the grasp of someone like Rex.

They sat in silence for several minutes, each silently praying that God would bring Eric back safe and sound. Suddenly, Dylan jumped out of his chair so quickly that the chair fell against the floor. "Carlie!"

Cassidy looked at him in surprise. "Carlie?" Had it suddenly hit him that his dog was missing?

"You said that Carlie was locked in Eric's room." Cassidy nodded. "That means that Eric didn't want Carlie following him so Rex didn't take him. He left and didn't want to take Carlie with him."

Relief filled Cassidy. Yes, her baby was missing, but at least he wasn't in the hands of someone who may harm him. "That makes sense although I still don't understand why he would leave, especially since he knew a storm was coming."

Dylan shrugged. "Your guess is as good as mine, but I bet that when Carlie dashed out of here, she was looking for Eric. Go check his room for a note or clothes missing – anything that might tell us he was running away." Dylan was hurriedly pulling on his jacket, hat, boots and gloves.

Cassidy ran up the stairs, nearly stumbling in her haste. She went over to the desk in Eric's room and saw that there was a note scrawled on a pad. She hurriedly read it, her heart racing.

> *Dear Mom,*
> *I thought that maybe you and Dylan would enjoy some time alone. I don't want to be a pest. I'm just going over to Wyatt's house. I'll probably spend the night because of the storm. I'll be back tomorrow.*
> *Love,*
> *Eric*

Cassidy tried not to grip on to the hope that was rising inside of her. She ripped the note from the pad and ran downstairs to Dylan. Thrusting it into his hand, she got out her phone and called over to the Clifford's house. As soon as they answered, she said, "Have you seen Eric? Is he there?"

"Warren brought him home earlier today, but we haven't seen him since," Karen answered. "Is everything okay?"

"He somehow got the idea that Dylan and I needed to be alone, and so he left a note saying that he was going to hang out with Wyatt." She knew her words were nearly incomprehensible in her alarm.

"Oh no! Let me ask Wyatt if he's seen him." Cassidy heard Karen speaking indistinctly for a moment before she got back on the phone. "I'm sorry, but Wyatt hasn't seen him either. If he shows up, we'll call you right away. And we'll be praying for him as well."

"Thank you." Cassidy hung up and turned haunted eyes to Dylan. "He's not there."

"I'm going out to look for him," Dylan pulled open the door. "We know which direction he was heading. Did Carlie run in the direction of the Clifford place?"

Cassidy took a moment to think back. "Yes, actually, she did."

"Then if we find Carlie, we'll find Eric."

"You think so?" She glanced at the window, at the swirl of white, and shook her head. "What are the chances that we could find them in this?" The tentative sprout of hope withered with despair.

Dylan gripped her arms. "Pray. Pray like you've never prayed before. Call the church. Ask them to get everyone praying. If we're going to find them, it's going to take a miracle. We need God on our side." He moved to the door. "While you're waiting, make sure that you have fresh warm clothes for Eric, a fire going, hot chocolate, blankets – anything. We'll need them when we get back." The door slammed behind him, and Cassidy stared at the door.

"God, I've lost so many people that I've loved already. Please don't take Eric and Dylan from me, too. Please protect them. Please." With her heart repeating that prayer over and over, Cassidy got to work to prepare things having faith that God would bring them back.

The Rescue

Dylan's heart sank as soon as he stepped off the porch. What were the chances of finding Eric and Carlie? With the snow and wind, it would be easy for Eric to get turned around and be unable to find his way home or to safety. In the cold, all alone, there were too many dangers for a boy.

"God, I need your help. I can't find him on my own, and he can't survive out there. Protect him. Guide me." Dylan plowed ahead, calling Carlie's name and Eric's alternately. The wind seemed to carry his voice straight back to him. At least he had a direction to begin looking. He knew where Eric was trying to go.

It didn't take long for his body to grow chilled. He hated to think about how Eric would be feeling after having been out for who knew how long. His own face was in pain from the cold, and he had only been out a short time.

Maybe Eric had found a neighbor's home. Maybe they hadn't called because the storm had knocked out the communications. Maybe he found a shelter and was keeping warm. He had to keep thinking these things as he struggled against the wind, forcing himself to move on.

Dylan wondered if he could find his own way back. How long should he search before he tried to head back? Maybe he should just keep going until he found a shelter of his own. What if he didn't find a shelter? Doubts and worries flooded his mind. The more he tried to push them aside, the more they infiltrated his thoughts. Finally he knelt in the snow. The wetness immediately penetrated his pants, but he hardly noticed.

"God, these worries aren't helping. You tell us not to worry about anything. Lord, I give Eric to You. Take away these worries and fears. Help me to focus on what's important." Feeling calmer, he climbed up from his knees and continued on.

Within a few minutes he heard a faint barking. His heart raced. He tried to tell himself that it could be any dog, but somehow he just knew it was Carlie. The other ranchers would have brought their dogs in out of this weather. He had heard stories about dogs who had kept children warm through blizzards, saving them from freezing to death. Perhaps Carlie had found Eric. He prayed that he would find them together.

Dylan followed the sound of the barking, stopping every once in a while to listen. Finally he saw something coming towards him. As soon as he recognized the black and white dog bounding toward him, he took off running toward her. His running felt slow and labored, but a burst of adrenaline helped him to continue. When Carlie realized that Dylan was following her, she turned around and took off in the opposite direction. After a few steps she turned to make sure he was following. Assured that he was coming, she gave a bark and continued on her way. Dylan picked up his pace to keep Carlie in his sight. He was certain that she knew where Eric was. His lungs hurt as he pushed his body to the limit.

A shadow loomed in front of him through the snow. Suddenly he was aware of exactly where he was. The Yoder ranch, the Rocking Y, had an old abandoned barn on the edge of their property. A decade ago they had rebuilt the barn closer to their home so that they wouldn't have to go as far in weather like this. They had opted to leave the old barn standing until it fell on its own. Normally he wouldn't consider the dilapidated building as a safe location for Eric to be, but at least it would provide some shelter from the elements.

He was thankful that Eric had seemed to keep a straight path. The fastest way to the Clifford's ranch would be to cut through the Rocking Y. He was certain that Eric and Wyatt had cut through the property multiple times before to see each other. The Yoder family wouldn't have minded. They may have even met up with the Yoder boys who were near Eric's age.

Carlie slipped throuh the door of the old barn which had a slight opening. Dylan pushed his shoulder against the door and forced it to open wider. The thought briefly crossed his mind that the whole building could collapse with the wind or the weight of the snow on the roof. He forced his mind onto other tracks as he entered the building that smelled of old hay and bat guano. Carlie dashed over to a corner where a boy was huddled, his shoulders shaking. When the dog reached him, Eric threw his arms around her neck and a sob tore through him.

"I thought you'd left me." Dylan's heart broke for the frightened child. "Why did you leave?" The sobs rose, growing in intensity.

Dylan crossed the floor purposefully. Eric heard his footsteps and raised his head, fear showing on his face. As he recognized Dylan, a mixture of relief and anxiety was visible in his expression.

"What are you doing here?" Eric hastily ran his coat sleeve across his face trying to erase the evidence of his tears.

"I'm looking for you, buddy." Dylan lowered himself to floor next to Eric. "What happened?"

Eric lowered his head. For a while, Dylan thought that he wouldn't respond at all, but eventually he heard his small voice. "I thought you and Mom didn't want me around."

"Why wouldn't we want you around?" Dylan searched in his mind for something he might have said or done that would make him think that he was in the way.

"Rex said that you guys would think I was in the way, because now that you're dating you'd want to be alone."

Dylan sighed heavily. "When did Rex say that?"

"When he was loading up the moving van and the truck with the trailer," Eric admitted.

It began to make sense. "You saw Rex loading up." It wasn't a question. Dylan knew that Rex wanted to get Eric away from the ranch so that he couldn't tell Cassidy what he had seen. "Did your mom or I ever make you feel like we didn't want you around?"

Eric thought for a moment. "No." His answer was soft and hesitant.

"That's because we care about you. When I asked your mom to begin dating me, I knew that you were part of that deal, and I loved it! My own mom was as excited to have you be part of the family as she was to have your mom."

Eric looked up at Dylan in disbelief. "Part of the family? But you're just dating. That doesn't make me part of the family."

"I consider you part of my family. If something happened where your mom and I could no longer be together, I would be sad to lose your mom, but I would also be sad to lose you." Dylan studied Eric for a moment. He knew that they needed to discuss it more, but he also needed to get Eric to warmth as quickly as possible. "Are you ready to go home?"

Eric nodded, tears filling his eyes. Dylan knew he was cold and scared. He needed his mother almost as much as he needed warmth right now. Dylan pulled out his cell phone and called Cassidy. She answered on the first ring, her eagerness and fear causing her voice to tremble.

"I found him. He's safe." She sobbed in relief, but he kept going. "I need you to do something so that we can both get home to you."

"Yes, of course." He could tell that she was trying to pull herself together.

"Go set off a flare. I need to know exactly where you are. We may be able to walk back." He went to the door of the barn. Remembering the angle that he had faced the barn as he approached it, he looked in the direction he had come.

"I just set it off." Her voice was breathless when she came back on. "Did you see it?"

He tightened his mouth. There was no way that he would be able to get Eric there. The boy would never make it. "I'm going to call the sheriff. I don't think we'll be able to walk, but maybe they can get a vehicle to us."

"Okay." He could hear the worry in her voice again. "I'll be praying you'll both be home soon. I love you both!"

Dylan felt his temperature rise. It was the first time that she had said she loved him, but there was no time to enjoy it. "We love you, too." He hung up and immediately dialed the police. Quickly explaining the situation, he told them his location.

"I've got help on the way. Remain where you are. Please stay on the line with me."

Dylan made his way back to the corner and wrapped his arm around Eric's shoulders. "They're on their way." He kept his voice soft.

"I'm so tired." Eric leaned into Dylan.

"I know you are, Buddy. We'll be home soon." It seemed like the wind was dying down. He hoped that the snow that was piled up wouldn't impede their progress too much. He worried that Eric was suffering from hypothermia. He held Eric close, willing his own body heat to warm the boy.

"Are you on the line?" A voice brought him to attention.

"Yes. How soon will they be here?"

"The blizzard has prevented travel by roads, but we have help on the way. Will you need medical assistance?"

Dylan looked down at Eric. "I think it would be a good idea to have someone check the boy out. He's been out in the cold for quite a while. But could we have them meet us at his house? I think getting him home would be the best for him and his mother."

"We'll get him home as soon as we can."

A whine of motors grabbed Dylan's attention. It didn't sound like cars or trucks, but it seemed like it was heading in his direction. He pulled away from Eric who had fallen asleep and went to the barn door. With the blizzard dying down, visibility had greatly improved. He saw some headlights off in the distance looking like fireflies. They were heading straight towards the barn. Dylan frowned. There weren't any roads from that direction.

"I see something," Dylan told the operator.

"What do you see?"

"Headlights. They're coming towards us."

"Looks like your help has arrived."

"How?" Dylan's brain tried to figure out what he was seeing, but his thought process was muddled. He knew the cold was affecting him as well as Eric. As he looked at his rescuers traveling towards him, his brow furrowed in thought. "Snowmobiles." It was almost a whisper, but the operator still heard him.

"Yes, sir. A direct way of travel in conditions like these. You're very lucky that the storm has let up so they could get to you so quickly."

"Not lucky," Dylan corrected. "We're very blessed."

There was a chuckle on the other end. "Yes, sir. Very blessed indeed."

The two snowmobiles were now nearing the door. Dylan disconnected and waved them over. They pulled nearby before turning off the motors and climbing off. They hurried into the barn. As they turned to Dylan, he saw that they were both in police uniforms. One was a male and the other female. The woman had a first aid kit in her hands.

Without speaking Dylan led them over to Eric. Carlie was curled up at his side, keeping him warm. The woman knelt beside Eric and felt for his pulse, took his temperature, and looked over his fingers. She nodded at her partner.

"He's a bit hypothermic, but no frost bite." She rubbed Carlie's head. "I'm sure that you helped keep him as warm as you could. Good dog!"

"It was the dog that got my attention and brought me to him." Dylan knelt beside Carlie and hugged her tightly.

"It was smart of him to find shelter," the male officer said. He glanced up at the holes in the roof. "Not sure this was the best shelter, but it protected him well enough."

"Let's get you guys home," the female officer said. She stood back and allowed the other officer to wrap Eric in a blanket and lift him up. Climbing on the snowmobile, she left room for Eric to be placed in front of her. The protective way she held him put any doubts that Dylan might have had to bed. Dylan picked up Carlie and headed to the other snowmobile. He climbed on the back clutching Carlie to his chest.

As Carlie whined, Dylan spoke softly in her ear. "Hold

on, girl. We'll be home soon."

The Homecoming

Cassidy paced the kitchen floor. She had every light in the house on, hoping to make it more obvious to anyone looking for it. Although she had thanked the Lord repeatedly that Dylan had found Eric and that he was safe, she knew that it would be difficult for them to get home still. As soon as she had heard from Dylan, she had called Karen and the pastor to let them know. She hadn't heard anything more since Dylan had hung up with her to call for emergency help. Pacing back to the window, she breathed a sigh of relief as she realized that the snow was slowing. The visibility clearing would make it much easier for them to find their way. She frowned as she noticed the amount of snow piled up around the house. What vehicle could possibly make it through that? Surely, they wouldn't have to walk back?

Cassidy jumped as her phone broke the silence. She hurried to answer it. Her heart sped up as she heard Clyde's voice.

"I wanted you to know that we stopped Rex and the truck of cattle at a roadblock. The truck driver was one of our guys so he led Rex right to us. With the theft of the cattle, we can take Rex in, but I think we have enough information now that we can press charges for the money issues as well. Rex was swearing so strongly that even his wife objected after awhile." The sheriff chuckled. "I think

175

we all learned some new vocabulary tonight."

Cassidy smiled. "Thank you so much. I'm glad it all worked out."

"Me, too." The sheriff cleared his throat. "Because of the weather, we couldn't get the cattle back to you tonight. I asked a neighboring rancher to take them for a day or two. I sort of implied that you would be happy to reimburse him for his time and feed and such."

"Of course, yes. I'll get them as soon as I possibly can, and I will be more than happy to pay him for his help." Two things surprised Cassidy. The first was that she had forgotten all about Rex. The second was that a rancher in the area believed that she would be trustworthy. She didn't know if that meant that the folks around here were starting to disbelieve the rumors, or if it meant that he trusted the sheriff's word, but she appreciated it in any case.

"I've heard on the radio that your boy's been found. Rex was cussing the boy for telling on him. It came out that Eric had caught Rex in the act, and to keep his secret, Rex had encouraged him to run away. I guess he told him that you and Dylan wanted to be alone. Thought you might be interested to know about that."

Cassidy lowered herself into a chair at the table. "Oh. Thank you. Yes, that makes sense."

"Eric and Dylan are on their way home, I've been told. Everyone is doing well, but Eric does have hypothermia so you'll need to get his body temperature back up."

"Hypothermia?" Cassidy felt like she'd been run over by a snowplow. Information was being dumped on her at an alarming rate. She was having trouble keeping up.

"He's going to be okay," the sheriff reassured her.

"Yes, of course." After thanking the sheriff, Cassidy hung up and immediately searched Google for how to help someone with hypothermia. She heated up some chicken broth, got some warm pajamas for him to change into, and got blankets ready. When she finished, she heard a commotion outside. Rushing to the door, she flung it open in time to see Dylan climbing off a snowmobile with a bundle in his arms. She stepped onto the porch, her feet unable to move further as she watched a man take another bundle from the woman on the second snowmobile.

The blanket fell away to reveal her son's precious face. Covering her mouth with her hand she lurched forward.

"He's okay," Dylan assured her. He placed his bundle down, and Carlie shook herself before going into the house. Dylan put his arm around her. "He's just sleeping. They've checked him over, and aside from mild hypothermia, he's okay."

Cassidy nodded, but tears fell down her cheeks as she watched the officer mount the porch under the weight of her son. As they entered the kitchen, Cassidy pulled her shoulders back and wiped her face. "Dylan, get coffee for the officers." She spoke to the officer carrying her son next. "Follow me." She led him into the living room and pointed to the couch. As soon as he set Eric down, the officer stood back and allowed Cassidy to take control. She helped him out of his wet clothes and into dry clothes, then placed a warm blanket around his shoulders. Eric's eyes opened, and his lips tipped up as he recognized his mother.

"Hi, Mom." He spoke softly, but it was the sweetest sound Cassidy could remember hearing.

"Hey, Buddy. Try to stay awake for me, okay?" Eric nodded, but his eyes slipped closed again.

She went back into the kitchen to find the officers sipping coffee, and Dylan drying off Carlie with a large towel. Hurrying over, she shook both of the officers' hands enthusiastically. "Thank you, thank you, thank you for bringing my son home to me!"

177

"It's our pleasure, ma'am," the female officer stated. "We're just pleased he's home safe."

Cassidy got a bowl of broth as the officers finished their coffee and headed back out on duty. Carlie trotted off when Dylan finished and rose to his feet. She quickly kissed him as she passed by. "I'm glad you're back safely, too. Get some coffee."

Dylan chuckled. "Yes, ma'am."

Entering the living room, Cassidy took a moment to look at the scene in front of her. The Christmas tree was lit, Carlie was asleep in front of the fire, and Eric was curled up on the couch looking young and vulnerable. She heard footsteps behind her and turned around. Dylan was clutching a coffee mug in his hands. He stopped beside her and surveyed the room as she had. "Looks like a peaceful Christmas scene, doesn't it?" He sipped his coffee and shook his head.

"It does." She walked over to Eric. "It is." She smiled at Dylan. "At least, now it is." She forced Eric to sit up, and eat some of the broth. After half a bowl, Eric was more alert, and looking stronger than he had when he had been brought in.

"I'm sorry, Mom." He blinked his eyes rapidly, trying to keep the tears back. "I thought you didn't want me around."

"I know, baby. The sheriff told me that Rex had suggested that Dylan and I needed alone time." She placed her hand on his cheek. "Honey, I love you and no man will ever replace you. If I didn't think that Dylan loved you as well as me, I wouldn't be with him."

"But grown-ups don't like kids around when they like each other."

Dylan came over and sat on the coffee table. "Sometimes they do like to be alone, but we can figure that out ourselves. We don't need you to leave for us."

"If we need alone time, we'll arrange for a date night or something. That's our responsibility, not yours." Cassidy brushed Eric's hair off his forehead. "But we do actually enjoy spending time with you as well."

Eric smiled. "Well, I am a pretty cool person," he joked.

Dylan laughed heartily. "Yes, you are." He stood and stretched. "I should go home."

Cassidy looked at him worriedly. "You can't leave, Dylan. The roads aren't clear. It would be unsafe for you to try."

Dylan shrugged. "I'll be okay."

"No, you're not leaving." Cassidy stood to her full height and folded her arms across her chest.

Dylan glanced between Cassidy and Eric who was watching the scene with widened eyes. "Cassidy, I'll be fine." His voice was softened, as if he were reasoning with someone that he doubted their mental stability.

Tears filled Cassidy's eyes. "I just got both of you back. I can't have you leave again, not knowing if you'll get home or not."

Dylan's eyes softened, and he rubbed her shoulders lovingly. "God will keep me safe. And if He doesn't, then that's okay, too." He lowered his voice. "I don't want to give the rumor mills anymore to talk about."

"You can sleep in my room," a small voice from the couch said. Dylan whipped around to face Eric. "I don't want you to leave either. It's not safe out there. The police had to use snowmobiles to come get us because it wasn't safe to be out on the roads. If they don't feel safe driving in that, then I don't feel like you should be out there either."

"People are going to talk about us," Cassidy added softly. "They'll talk about how and why Eric ran away. They'll talk about Rex and the cattle. They'll talk about our relationship. I don't care anymore. If they want to know the truth, they can ask. If not," she shrugged, "then they have to answer to God."

Dylan looked between the two of them. "I don't know."

Cassidy sensed his resolve weakening. "Eric will sleep with me tonight. You can sleep in his room. Tomorrow we'll see how the roads are."

"I don't have to kick Eric out of his room. I can make my way over to the foreman's house. It's not far and with the storm passed, I won't have any difficulty making it."

"Then it's settled. Time for bed, Eric." She put her arm around her son's shoulders and headed up the stairs.

"Good night." Cassidy turned around halfway up the staircase. Dylan stood at the foot of the stairs, one hand on the railing, the other in his pocket. Cassidy smiled. With her arm around her son and the man she loved nearby, she felt like this could be the best Christmas she'd ever had.

"Sweet dreams," she answered, and she knew that hers would be very sweet indeed.

The Christmas Celebration

Christmas morning dawned sparkling white with the snow from the blizzard. It was beautiful, cold, and perfect. Cassidy smiled softly as she ran down the stairs. Her son was safe at home, Rex was gone, Dylan was here, and it was Christmas day. What could be better?

She had dressed carefully in a red sweater and jeans, curled her long dark hair and carefully applied her make-up before heading to the kitchen. She got coffee going and then bundled up to take care of her chickens. Gratitude filled her knowing that her cattle were being taken care of, and that she didn't have to worry about that on such a frigid morning. She made a mental note to slip in some extra money to thank the rancher for caring for her cows, not only after a blizzard, but on Christmas day as well.

When she got back from tending the chickens, the coffee was finished. She poured herself a cup and got to work on breakfast. After the night they had, she felt that something special was in order. The bacon had cooked to a crisp and the last slice of egg nog french toast had been placed on the platter when Dylan stepped into the kitchen from the back porch.

His sandy hair was wet from a recent wash and he had a day's growth of stubble on his chin. He got out of his coat and boots before coming over to where she was still standing by the stove. Cassidy felt butterflies in her stomach when he smiled. "Merry Christmas." His voice was still rough with sleep. He came over and kissed her tenderly. "I thought I smelled bacon."

She laughed. "A surefire way to get a man – cook bacon."

Dylan smiled as he poured his own cup of coffee. "Coffee is a pretty good way, too."

A thundering sound filled the house as Eric and Carlie barreled down the stairs and tumbled into the kitchen. "It's Christmas! Can I check my stocking out before breakfast?"

Cassidy smiled broadly. Sometimes Eric seemed so grown up. It was nice to see the little boy in him still make appearances. "I suppose that would be okay, but you need to care for Carlie first."

Eric pulled out a bowl and filled it with the dog food that was left over from when she had lived with them before. He hurried through the chore and then ran into the living room. Carlie looked after him as if debating whether to follow or not, but sustenance won out.

Cassidy and Dylan followed Eric and got there just as he was pulling out the first item. He exclaimed eagerly over each new discovery, but the event was over quickly. The group went back to the kitchen where they enjoyed the breakfast that Cassidy had prepared. Eric had wolfed down his food in record time. He shoved his chair back. "Presents, now?"

Cassidy laughed. "Dylan and I are still eating. Besides I need to get things ready for lunch. Why don't you go upstairs and get dressed? It won't hurt you to wait. You'll have everything opened before lunch and then there won't be any anticipation left."

"Yeah, but there will be toys." In spite of his protest,

Eric went back upstairs to get dressed.

Dylan and Cassidy finished eating and cleaned up the kitchen. Dylan kissed her neck and whispered, "Maybe we should have Christmas dinner instead of lunch. I'm stuffed."

Cassidy smiled as she wrapped her arms around him. "Probably not a bad idea. We'll have to see if the boy who is growing like a weed can hold out that long."

"I'm sure we can keep him occupied." Dylan searched her face for a long moment. "I don't want to scare you or anything, but this feels – natural. It feels like we're a family."

Cassidy nodded. "I was thinking the same thing. It's sort of strange."

"I like it."

"Me, too." Cassidy smiled up at him. "Now, you'd better leave so I can get some of this food prepared for later."

"I should probably call my mom. She'll want to know what happened last night." Dylan pulled his phone out of his pocket and was dialing his mom's number as he left the kitchen.

It didn't take long for Cassidy to prepare the turkey and get it in the oven. Most of the other dishes would be put in the oven shortly before they ate. She had tried to keep dinner simple, but festive. With only three of them, she didn't want a bunch of leftovers. Yet she still wanted it to feel like Christmas.

Eric came bursting into the living room the same time as she did. His hair was wetted down and Cassidy was amused to see that he had tried to style it like Dylan's. Eric threw himself on the couch next to Dylan who chuckled at the boy's enthusiasm. He handed the phone to Eric. "My mom wants to wish you a Merry Christmas."

Eric eagerly grasped the phone and began chatting eagerly, telling her all about his adventure from the night before. Dylan went and got the fireplace going while Cassidy took a seat on the couch. "I thought he might enjoy telling others about his adventure," Dylan said with a smile.

Cassidy shivered as she remembered the anxiety that she had suffered through as she had waited for Eric to come home. "I'm just glad it's over and that he's safe."

Dylan came over to sit next to her. He placed his arm around her shoulders. "I am, too. By the way, Mom's glad you made me stay here last night."

Cassidy looked up at him and noticed his eyes were twinkling. "Oh, why's that?"

"Well, first, because it shows that you were concerned about my safety. You understand as a mother that is very important in a future daughter-in-law." Cassidy started to sputter, but Dylan kept talking. "Second, it meant that I could be with you and Eric on Christmas. If I hadn't stayed here, I probably would have been stuck at home all alone on Christmas. That would make her feel guilty for leaving me alone on a holiday, and she'd never be able to leave again. Thirdly, it means that I have to make an honest woman of you."

Cassidy nearly choked. "But I'm not . . . we didn't . . . nothing happened!"

Dylan laughed at her horror. "We know that, and she knows that, but the town," he left the sentence hanging for her to fill in.

Cassidy covered her face. "Oh my goodness!"

Dylan squeezed her shoulders. "Don't worry about it. I think that it will blow over quickly. With Rex's arrest, it might not even get noticed. Let's just enjoy the day."

Eric came back in and handed the phone to Cassidy. "She wants to talk to you." He rolled his eyes. "We're never going to get to open presents."

"Eric!" Cassidy admonished her son before taking the phone. "Why don't you pass out the gifts while you wait for me?" Eric hurried to obey his mom, and Cassidy settled back on the couch. "Hi, Jean! How's Arizona?"

"A lot different from what you're experiencing I hear," Jean laughed. "It's sixty degrees here, and they're talking about how cold it is."

Cassidy laughed. "I suppose they're not used to those temperatures."

"I'm so disappointed that I missed all the excitement," Jean continued. "I wanted to be there when Rex got picked up." The dismay in Jean's voice made Cassidy burst out laughing.

"Well, if it makes you feel better, we all missed it. We were a little more concerned about Eric at that time." Cassidy looked over at her son and once more gave thanks that he was there to celebrate with them. "I'm so glad Dylan was here. I don't know what I would have done without him." Carlie looked up at her from her place in front of the fire, making Cassidy chuckle. "And Carlie, too. She saved Eric's life."

"I'm glad Dylan and Carlie were there, too. Although I have to say that from what I know of you, you would have been just fine on your own. You're stronger than you think." There was some noise in the background. "I have to go. Apparently it's time to open gifts. Have a Merry Christmas and thank you."

"For what?"

"For taking care of my boy. He needs you." With that, Jean hung up.

Cassidy handed the phone back to Dylan, and Eric sat up eagerly. "Now?" The excitement radiating from him was contagious.

"Yes, now." Cassidy couldn't remember enjoying a Christmas more since she was a child herself. Seeing her son enthusiastically open his gifts, showing gratitude for each one, and knowing that she could have easily lost him made this day precious. The arm around her shoulders was a reminder of the love she had found, the support that Dylan had shown her, and the second chance God was giving her.

******

Dylan loaded up his gifts into his truck. His mom had left him a gift which had turned out to be a standing tool box, and Cassidy had given him a new Stetson. He had been surprised by a gift from Eric though. He had given Dylan a framed picture of himself and Carlie. Dylan had promised that he would put the picture in his office so he would see them both every day.

Although Dylan wasn't worried about the possible rumors his stay at the Golden Creek Ranch might incite, he was glad that the roads had been cleared sufficiently for him to get back home. He didn't want Cassidy to have to go through that experience again. He walked back up the porch steps to where Cassidy was standing in her coat. Eric was already in bed, so they had a moment alone.

"Thank you again for the necklace," she said, fingering the gold cross at her neck.

"You're very welcome. Thanks for taking care of me, and for the hat."

"You're welcome." She smiled up at him. "I'm glad you were here to celebrate with us."

Dylan pulled her into his arms and kissed her. "I love you, Cassidy. I feel like I've known you so much longer than I have. I know that we still need to get to know each other more, but I want you to know that I'm serious about

186

us."

Cassidy sighed. "I love you, too. And I love you even more for everything you just said."

Dylan smiled. "I really do feel like we're already family, and I do feel like we have a future. I want you to know that."

"But it's better to make absolutely certain. I've already had one bad marriage. I don't want to go through that again."

Dylan held her tightly. "I don't want to hurt you."

"I know. It's been a long time since I've trusted anyone, but I trust you."

"I'd better get going. It's getting hard for me to leave." He chuckled. "You'll get tired of seeing me around here."

"I somehow doubt that."

Epilogue

SNOWFALL, WYOMING
Christmas Day, two years later

Cassidy slowly opened her eyes. The weak sunlight that came in through the curtains told her that the sun was only just peaking over the horizon. She rolled over in bed and looked at Dylan's face. After a year of marriage, she was still amazed that he was her husband.

His eyes blinked open and he smiled lazily. "How long have you been staring at me?"

"Long enough to be thankful for such a handsome husband."

He growled and pulled her against him. "Not nearly as thankful as I am for my lovely wife. Happy anniversary, Mrs. Thompson."

"Happy anniversary and Merry Christmas to you." She kissed him softly.

"You have to admit, getting married on Christmas was genius. I'll never forget our anniversary." He chuckled.

"Yes, darling, you're absolutely brilliant." She ran her hand through his hair. As she leaned forward to kiss him again, a cry pierced the morning quiet. She groaned. "I'll get the princess."

"I'll get coffee going," Dylan promised.

"That would be lovely," Cassidy sighed.

"I'm telling you, you hit the jackpot when you married me."

"Be careful that your head still fits through the door before you leave the bedroom," she teased kissing him once more before climbing out of bed. She went across the hallway and entered the baby nursery. "Elicia Jean, what is all this fuss about? Are you ready for breakfast already?" The month old baby girl blinked up at her mother for a moment before letting out another wail. Cassidy picked up her daughter, changed her and took her to the rocking chair to nurse. As Cassidy had come to expect, Carlie came padding in and positioned herself near the chair, keeping an eye on the baby. She had quickly become Elicia's protector.

Eric stuck his head in the door. The two years that had passed had made a significant change in her son. Now fourteen, he had grown several inches and his deepening voice let her know that her boy was becoming a man. "I thought I heard Elicia," he said.

"You did. She just needs to be fed. We'll be down soon." Cassidy had been amazed at how much Eric loved and doted on his baby sister.

"I'll go help with breakfast." She heard him racing down the stairs, but now Carlie didn't follow at his heels.

As she rocked her daughter her mind drifted back in time. The news of Rex's arrest had eclipsed any notice of Eric's running away or Dylan staying the night. She had happily repaid the rancher who had taken care of her cows during the blizzard. He had even bought a large portion of her herd later in the spring, and this time there was nothing suspicious about the amount. She had been able to build the guest houses on her property for the guest ranch that summer and opened for business in the fall. That summer, Dylan had also decided that it was time for them to officially become a family. He had proposed with Eric's approval and assistance and together the three of them had decided on a Christmas wedding.

The wedding had been small. The Cliffords, Jean, and Eric had gathered at the church in the evening where the pastor had graciously agreed to marry them. Cassidy had been relieved that he had been willing to interrupt his own Christmas to take time for the service. Eric had spent a week with Jean while Dylan and Cassidy had enjoyed their honeymoon and when they came back they found him referring to her as "Grandma Jean". Dylan had officially adopted Eric shortly after and as soon as it was official Eric began calling him "Dad".

Only a few short months after the wedding, Cassidy had found she was expecting. The family had eagerly prepared for the arrival of Elicia and spoiled Cassidy. As Cassidy looked down at her baby, she was amazed once again at all that had happened. Even the rumors that had plagued her had disappeared once Rex had been arrested. Most people in town had told her that they had never believed the gossip, but Cassidy no longer cared about what they had thought. She was just relieved that she finally felt like she belonged.

By the time she had Elicia dressed in her Christmas outfit, the baby was asleep again. Cassidy took the opportunity to dress in jeans and forest green blouse. She hurriedly french braided her long hair and headed downstairs. Dylan and Eric had breakfast ready by the time she came in.

"Where's Elicia?" Eric asked.

"She fell back asleep so I put her back in her crib."

"Mom! It's her first Christmas, and she's missing it!"

"Eric, she's a baby. She's not going to remember it anyway. I promise that whether she is sleeping or not I will have her with us when we open gifts."

Dylan patted Eric on the shoulder. "I'm excited about her first Christmas, too, but let's allow your mom to enjoy her Christmas breakfast."

"Okay, Dad." Eric's attention fell to his food, but Cassidy felt a familiar warmth whenever she heard him refer to Dylan as "dad". It had happened naturally, but she knew that it meant the world to Dylan.

As they were finishing up the dishes, a car pulled into the drive. Cassidy was thankful that there was snow, but that it wasn't the blizzard conditions they had experienced two years ago.

"Grandma Jean is here!" Eric bolted out the door and down the porch steps to help Jean carry the gifts and food into the house.

Dylan laughed. "I'll go help. You should get the baby. Mom is going to want to hold her as soon as she gets in the house."

Cassidy smiled and shook her head. If they managed to keep this little girl from being spoiled rotten it would be a miracle.

"Where's my granddaughter?" Cassidy wasn't sure if the door had even closed behind Jean before she voiced the question.

"She's right here," Cassidy answered as she reached the bottom of the stairs. She passed Elicia off to her mother-in-law who had her arms eagerly outstretched for the baby.

"There's my precious Elicia Jean." She rarely didn't use the baby's full name, a sign of how tickled she was about her namesake. "Grandma has missed you so much."

"You saw her last night, Mom." Dylan found amusement in his mom's enthusiasm for her granddaughter.

"I'm still allowed to miss her." Jean sat down in the recliner and made cooing noises at the sleeping baby.

"We're thankful she has such a doting grandma so

close," Cassidy assured her.

It wasn't long before Eric insisted it was time for gifts. Jean handed Elicia back to Cassidy so that she could take pictures. Cassidy sat back and watched the scene in front of her. The fire in the fireplace, the Christmas tree with its lights lit, the gifts scattered around the room, Eric's excited face, Jean snapping pictures, Dylan directing everything, and the tiny bundle in her arms – it was everything that she had always dreamed of.

Dylan sank onto the couch beside her and put his arm around her. He bent over and kissed their daughter's head. He looked up into his wife's face and frowned. "You're crying. Is everything all right?"

"Everything is perfect," she answered softly. Dylan smiled and kissed her tenderly.

"Yes, it is. God has been so good to us."

Dear Reader,

A few years ago we were traveling from Arizona to Minnesota for a family reunion. We had made it a road trip, so we got to see several states. This was my first time to see the state of Wyoming. As we traveled through, I saw in my mind an image of a woman standing on a porch with her son. That was the very beginning of this story.

Last year, I took a year off from writing a Christmas novella, and I had some requests that I write another one. So I made it one of my goals for the year to publish one for Christmas. It seemed like it was time to pull this story out and write it down.

I had some trouble piecing this one together. I think my first version seemed like something out of a western and not very likely to occur in present time. Fortunately, my sister-in-law, Rachel Lyman, lives in a ranching community, and I was able to use her knowledge to help make it more realistic. I'm so grateful for her assistance.

Christmas isn't always a cheerful season for everyone. There are times of pain and grief, times of difficulty, and times of discouragement. Even in the midst of all of these things, there can still be joy. I pray that your Christmas will be filled with joy this year.

MERRY CHRISTMAS!
Courtney Lyman

Made in the USA
Middletown, DE
23 August 2022

71306986R00118